The Shy Ones

Other titles by
Lynn Hall

GENTLY TOUCH THE MILKWEED	49353	1.50
NEW DAY FOR DRAGON	30528	1.25
RIDE A WILD DREAM	40303	1.50
RIFF, REMEMBER	21899	.95
THE SIEGE OF SILENT HENRY	49445	1.50
STRAY	23473	.95
TROUBLEMAKER	26203	1.25

The Shy Ones
Lynn Hall

Illustrated by Greta Elgaard

AN AVON CAMELOT BOOK

AVON BOOKS
A division of
The Hearst Corporation
959 Eighth Avenue
New York, New York 10019

First Camelot Printing, October, 1977
Fifth Printing

Printed in the U.S.A.

FOR BRAEWICKE'S KLONDIKE KATE,

a champion in every way

LYNN HALL's interest in animals started in her childhood and continues into her adult life. Among other jobs, she has worked as a veterinarian's assistant and an assistant handler on dog show circuits.

Ms. Hall based the character of Kate, the dog in this story, on a golden retriever that was given to her as an alternative to putting it to sleep for excessive shyness. She worked with the dog for one summer and then showed her in five dog shows. Braewicke's Klondike Kate won her classes at each show, coming within two points of completing her championship in nearly record time. Kate now is "a fat and happy children's pet" in a small Iowa town.

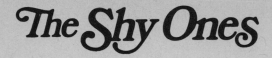

The Shy Ones

ONE

Saturday morning. Robin woke slowly, inch by inch, savoring the delicious no-school feeling. No need this morning to force her eyes open until they were ready to open. She rolled over to lie face down, toes hooked over the foot of the bed, hands dangling from either side, her nose pressed against the sheet. As usual, she had lost her pillow during the night.

Someone, probably her father, was working in the yard under her open window. Through the hiss of the lawn sprinkler, Robin could hear the slow chunking of a spade in the dirt. She couldn't hear anything from the kitchen under her room, so evidently breakfast was over and the dishes done already. It was probably the middle of the morning. She knew she'd be headachy the rest of the day if she stayed in bed too long, but it felt so good just to lie there and let her mind wander.

Last night had been pretty bad. Awful, in fact Sock hops were supposed to be fun. Casual, happy, everybody dancing and having a ball. Well, she'd gone. Full of optimism, she had walked to the gym with Marilyn and Darlene, checked her loafers at the door with everybody else, and padded on into the streamer-hung basketball court, feeling foolish in her stocking feet.

Robin decided not to think about the sock hop any more. About how much she had looked forward to it, deciding a dozen times what to wear and hoping that *this* dance would be different. But it hadn't been any better than the junior high dances, or the get-acquainted dance at the first of this year. A few more boys had braved the trip across the floor this time to dance with a girl, but not with Robin Morgan. Still not with her.

She had stood along the wall beside the bleachers with Marilyn and Darlene, making stiff, desperate conversation so people would think they weren't dancing because they preferred to talk. But there was really nothing to say. The endless hours had been broken only by hair-combing trips and long silences while the three girls tried not to look around the room as though waiting to be asked to dance.

Robin flopped over or her back, eyes still shut tight. Only two dances all evening. Two lousy dance and both with boys that nobody else liked. And Dwight hadn't asked her to dance at all. What a relief when it was time to go home. And what a letdown.

Reaching under the bed, Robin fished out her glasses. She poked them on and raised the window shade beside the bed. At least it was going to be a beautiful day, warm and fresh and cloudless. The lilac bush that reached almost to her windowsill was loaded with blooms. Pushing out the screen, she reached down and broke off one of the lacy purple cones. She cupped her hands around it and buried her nose in the tiny blossoms.

"Robin, are you up yet?" Her mother's voice reminded her that time was wasting.

"Just getting."

"Eggs?"

"No thanks. I'll fix myself something." She laid the lilac carefully on the dresser, then pulled on jeans and a plaid blouse and clomped down the stairs, buttoning her blouse as she went.

Mrs. Morgan was moving things around in the living room, getting ready to vacuum. "Have a good time last night?" she asked.

"Oh yeah, it was lots of fun." Robin went into the kitchen and started a piece of toast. She didn't want to tell her mother what a wallflower she had been, and have to listen to the little talk about how Nobody

11

Ever Gets Over Being Shy Without Making An Effort. She just wanted to forget the whole thing and not mess up a nice Saturday thinking about Dwight Wolber.

After breakfast Robin carried out all the waste-baskets and burned their contents in the trash barrel at the back of the yard. Then, armed with dust mop and cloth, she began on her room. She poked the mop around, not going too far under the bed, then swept the dust down the stairs for her mother to take from there.

As she stood on the bottom step, gently shaking the mop over the little pile of dust, she saw herself in the long mirror on the coat closet door. Robin Louise Morgan, you're a mess, she thought, sighing. No, not really a mess, just so gosh-darned ordinary! Medium size, medium shape. Medium brown hair, medium long. Ugly pinkish glasses that hid eyes that were really pretty good.

She leaned the dust mop against the wall and stood close to the mirror, taking off her glasses and holding her eyes wide open so they really did look big. She tilted her head back and smiled a Mona Lisa smile, her eyes half closed. Then she sighed again, put the glasses back on, and went to find her mother.

"Mom, I guess I'll take a picnic lunch out to McNeal Park if you don't care. I'll just loaf around out there this afternoon."

"Sure, dear; if your room's done, go on."

Addy Morgan looked after Robin as the girl started making her peanut butter and jelly sandwich. Things must not have gone too well at the dance, Robin was so quiet this morning. Not that she was ever a noisy girl. Addy often wished her daughter were a little noisier. Or, more precisely, not so closed in on herself all the time. At fifteen, Robin should be having a few dates or bringing friends to the house. The older Robin got, the harder it was to reach her. The forty years difference between them was just too much.

Robin dropped her sandwich and an orange into a paper bag, called good-bye to her mother, and went out the back door and across the porch that covered three sides of the rambling yellow house. Standing in the shelter of the porch, she watched her father cross the yard toward the old garage that had originally been a small barn. He looks so old, in his overalls and gray hair, she thought. More like a grandfather than a father.

She didn't mean the thought disloyally. Robin loved her parents, but it was so embarrassing, when kids asked what her father did, to say he was retired —especially when so many of them had young, fun parents. If hers were younger, it might be easier to talk to them about things.

She got her bike out of the garage, passing her father on the way. They exchanged good mornings, and she pedaled down the driveway, her lunch sack bouncing in the basket.

Instead of heading west on Maple, toward the park, Robin turned first toward downtown and the library. It would be a good day to sit out in the park and read. She leaned her bike against the gray stone of the library building and went inside.

Since it was Saturday, there was a long line at the check-out desk. Robin chose a book, then kept its title hidden while she waited her turn in line. It was on personality development for teen-agers. She knew before she read it what it would say. If you're shy, think of others instead of yourself. Get your mind off how shy you are and you won't be shy anymore. But the vicious circle wasn't that easy to break. She'd tried, and she knew. Still, this book might tell her something that would kind of start things rolling.

She dropped the book into her bike basket and started back out Maple. McNeal Park was outside of town, about a mile beyond the Cedar Grove city limits. It was a pleasant ride out there, with no big hills to climb, and the stretch of Maple Street between the edge of town and the park was deeply shaded and little traveled.

Pedaling along this quiet part of the road, Robin dropped her hands from the handlebars and let her arms hang limp. Her body guided the bike, the slightest shift of weight swaying it from side to side. She and the bike were a pair of ballet dancers. Or the bike was a beautiful horse, so sensitive he needed no reins to guide him.

Suddenly Robin grabbed the handlebars and slammed on the brakes. There was something in the ditch back there. She let the bike drop beside the road and went back through the weeds along the bank. There it was, almost hidden in the long grass. A big yellow furred mound . . . a dog.

TWO

Robin leaned over the dog. It was lying frighteningly still, eyes closed, but when she touched it, the fur was warm and the ribs were moving gently up and down. It was alive.

She knew she shouldn't try to move the dog even if she were able to, but she couldn't just leave the poor thing there. A farmhouse was just down the road, and Robin got her bike and pedaled toward it as fast as she could, her heart pounding. That poor thing, she thought. Somebody must have hit it with his car and left it there.

She knocked at the farmhouse door and asked the tall hawk-faced woman who answered if they owned a big yellow dog.

"No," the woman said, drying her hands on her apron. "We haven't had a dog in years. Why?"

"There's one down by the road. It's been hurt, but it's still alive." Robin's voice was shaky. "Do you know anybody around here that it might belong to?"

The woman shook her head but held open the door. "You're welcome to use the phone, though, if you want to call the police or a vet."

Robin followed her through the cluttered, dark living room to the telephone, then stood staring at it, undecided. Probably she should call a veterinarian. Right now it was more important to get the dog taken care of than to find out who it belonged to.

Of the two veterinarians in Cedar Grove, only one bothered with dogs and cats—Dr. Cook, who had put Cindy, the Morgans' ancient cocker spaniel, to sleep two years ago. Robin looked up his number and dialed. Luckily, he was in.

"Hello, Doctor. There's a dog that's been hit out here, about half a mile past the end of Maple. Could you come and get it. . . . No, I don't know who it belongs to, but I think it's hurt pretty bad. . . . Oh, good. I'll wait for you there, just before where the park starts. And thank you very much!"

Robin thanked the woman and rode off, pumping furiously. What if the dog were already dead? Or had gotten up and moved off somewhere?

17

But it was still there. Robin sat in the dusty grass beside the dog's yellow head, stroking it and watching with apprehension for any changes in the breathing. Tears stung in her nose as she looked the dog over more closely. It was painfully thin, with crusts of dried mud plastered to its legs.

Robin saw, with a sick shock, that one foreleg was bent grotesquely forward. The skin wasn't broken, but the angle of the leg showed clearly that the bone was. Robin looked away quickly and wished Dr. Cook would get there.

In a matter of minutes a dusty red station wagon stopped beside Robin, and the veterinarian got out and came around to kneel beside the dog. He pressed one hand against its ribs, under the forelegs, then flipped up a lip to reveal gums that were startlingly pale. Gently, he ran his hands over the rest of the gaunt yellow body.

"Would you get that wide board out of the car, and the blanket?" It was the first notice he had taken of Robin. She jumped up and got them.

Between them, they wrapped the old baby blanket around the dog and eased the mound onto the board. Carefully they slid the board into the back of the station wagon. Robin got her lunch and book and climbed into the car beside the dog. They turned around in the farm lane and headed back toward town.

"How bad do you think . . ."

"Hard to say yet," Dr. Cook said. "She's in shock, and of course the leg's broken. But whether there's any internal damage, we'll just have to wait to find out." He was a young man, with close-cropped wiry black hair and heavy eyebrows that nearly ran together over deep-set blue eyes.

Robin kept a hand on the dog's head all the way back, talking softly to her, wanting to get through her unconsciousness to let her know that everything was going to be all right now.

Dr. Cook's clinic was a small white concrete block building at the back of his house, which was on the corner of Third and Maple, just a few blocks west of Robin's house. He parked the car beside the clinic, and he and Robin carried their blanket-wrapped burden inside to be laid, board and all, on the stainless steel table in the tiny examining room.

Dr. Cook washed his hands, put on a clean white wraparound, and began a thorough examination of the dog while Robin stood out of his way and watched.

"She's a golden retriever, isn't she?" Robin asked.

"Mm-hmm. Poor thing's so thin and dirty it's hard to tell, but she's a golden all right. Not a bad one either, I'd say." He left the room and returned with two square metal plates, silver and black, which he handed to Robin.

"You'll have to help me, if you don't mind. My wife usually does, but she's not feeling too hot today, so I gave her the day off. I want to get X rays of

19

that leg while she's still in shock and won't fight us."

He wheeled a large black machine out from the corner and positioned it next to the table so that it loomed over the dog. From a drawer he took two heavy leaded aprons and two pairs of lead gloves, which he and Robin put on. Then, very carefully he rolled the dog, whose head was moving groggily now, onto her other side so the injured leg was on the table. Gently he slid one of the metal plates under the leg until the broken place was centered on the plate.

He placed one of Robin's gloved hands on the good leg to keep it out of the way of the X ray, and her other hand on the dog's neck to quiet her feeble attempts to get up. Then he adjusted some knobs on the back of the machine and pressed a button. There was a buzz-click, and it was done.

"Now the hard part," he said. "We'll have to get one front view of the bone." Very gently he rolled the dog over, tucking in her hind legs, until her head was up and both forelegs were out in front of her. Robin held the lolling head to one side while the second picture was taken, wincing inside when the leg had to be moved.

But finally it was done, and the dog was laid in a clean cage in the back room. Dr. Cook had wrapped the dog's leg in a temporary splint and had given her a shot of penicillin and a pain-killer before putting her in the cage.

"That's all we can do for now," he said, untying his white coat. "There doesn't seem to be anything else broken, and I can't set that leg till she comes out of shock. The best thing for her now is to be left alone in a warm dark place. By tomorrow, if she hasn't been injured internally, she should be in good enough shape to take the anesthetic for the bone setting. Now let's see if we can find out who owns her."

Robin followed Dr. Cook to the reception room and watched while he rifled through a file drawer full of small white cards. He pinched his lips between his fingers and frowned.

"Let's see, let's see . . . golden retrievers. Who's got a golden retriever around here? Petersens, but this isn't their dog. Maybe Carter Crissman would know." He reached for the phone.

"Who's Carter Crissman?"

"He has a kennel out south of town about three miles. On Highway 68. You've probably seen it— that nice brick house that sits way back from the road? He raises golden retrievers—show dogs. He's got some good ones out there. I'm sure this isn't one of his, as thin as she is, but . . . Hello, Carter? Tom Cook."

While Dr. Cook talked, Robin looked around the room. It was small but bright and clean, with tan tile floors and white walls, and two large windows looking out on Third Avenue. The only furnishings

21

were the reception desk in the corner, fenced off on two sides by a high counter, a few modern-looking chairs, and a small metal table covered with magazines. In one corner a rubber plant grew almost to the ceiling.

" . . . You bet. Thanks, Carter. Nice to talk to you." Dr. Cook hung up and turned to Robin. "He didn't know of anyone hereabouts losing a golden, but he said he'd ask around. I suppose we should check with the police next."

Robin nodded, leaning against the counter while he dialed again. Surely someone had reported a lost dog. Even if she was thin and dirty, she was still a purebred, Dr. Cook had said. They were bound to be looking for her. Still, if they didn't take any better care of their dog than that, Robin wasn't sure they deserved to have her back.

But no one had reported a missing golden retriever to the police. Dr. Cook left his phone number and the dog's description, and hung up.

"Well, young lady, looks like the only thing for you to do is put an ad in next week's *Messenger* and see if anybody calls to claim her."

"What if nobody does?" Robin asked, running her thumbnail along the edge of the counter.

"Well then, I guess she'd be your responsibility."

Her responsibility. Her dog. She thought of the animal lying in the cage in the back room, groggy with pain, maybe dying. She tried to picture her well

22

and lively, bones covered with muscle, golden coat brushed and gleaming. Robin Morgan's beautiful purebred golden retriever. If only nobody claims her . . . If only she doesn't die . . .

Dr. Cook cleared his throat. "I hate to bring up an ugly subject like money, but if no one claims her—well, there will be expenses, setting the leg and all."

Robin lifted her chin and looked him in the eye. "Don't worry, Dr. Cook. I'll be responsible. Could I see her again before I go?"

They went through the narrow hall to the big back room. Cages connected to outdoor runs lined one wall, and a triple tier of smaller cages lined the opposite side. The retriever was in the last of these, in the bottom row.

Robin kneeled and opened the cage door. The dog's head was weaving weakly, just off the cage floor, but her eyes still had a glazed look, and she didn't respond at all when Robin reached in and touched a silky ear.

Robin closed the door and stood up. "How early tomorrow can I come and see how she is?"

Dr. Cook laughed. "Not before nine, please. I like to sleep a little later on Sunday when I can. We should know by then if she's going to come out of it."

Robin thanked him and left, nearly forgetting to get her lunch and library book out of the station wagon. She walked the three blocks home, automatically dodging roller skaters and tricyclists, and trying to imagine what her parents were going to say about all this.

They were both on the back porch when she got home, sitting on the glider with a nursery catalog between them.

"Hi," Robin said, dropping to the top step to sit with her back to the railing.

"Back from the park already, dear?" Mrs. Morgan marked her place in the catalog with a finger and looked up. "I didn't hear your bike."

"I didn't get to the park." She took a deep breath. "Something happened on the way."

She had their attention immediately, and she told the story quickly, glossing over the possibility of veterinary bills to be dealt with.

"Haven't you sort of put yourself out on a limb, Robin?" her father asked, not unkindly. "If nobody claims the dog, what will you do?"

"I'll pay the doctor bill myself," she said defensively. "I couldn't just leave the poor thing to die."

Her mother frowned a practical little frown. "Where did you plan to get the money? Setting a broken bone, and all those X rays, that's going to mount up, you know."

"I know. I'll earn the money some way. Don't worry." The words came out sharper than she had intended them.

"Did you plan to keep the dog, then?"

Robin looked from one parent to the other. "I sure do want to, if I can."

There was a long, heavy pause. Then Mrs. Morgan said, "You know what we decided after Cindy was put to sleep, Robin. No more dogs. You just get attached to them and something happens. You remember how we all felt about Cindy. . . ." She still found it hard to talk about the cocker.

Robin turned to her father, her eyes begging. He harrumphed. "It might be all right, Addy—if Robin wants to do all the work of taking care of the dog. Might be good company for her. Besides, someone's bound to claim it sooner or later."

Robin wanted to jump up and hug her father, but they weren't much of a family for hugging, so she said instead, "I'll do all the work and pay for the dog food, and I won't let her dig up the yard." Her voice was light, and she bounced up from the step. "Would one of you have time to drive me out to get my bike?"

All three Morgans drove off to retrieve the bicycle, and the book on personality development lay forgotten on the porch.

THREE

A few minutes before nine the next morning, Dr. Cook looked out his kitchen window and saw Robin sitting on the curb in front of the clinic. She jumped up when he crossed his backyard toward her.

"Morning," he called across the yard. "Have you had the mumps?"

"Yes, both sides. Why?"

He came closer then. "Just checking. My wife's got them, and both of the kids. I didn't want to be bringing you any little germs. Shall we go in and see how our patient looks this morning?" He unlocked the door and led the way to the back room.

She might be dead, Robin cautioned herself. She might be . . .

But she wasn't. The retriever was crouched against the back of the cage, her splinted leg protruding awkwardly. Robin kneeled in front of the cage and looked through the bars, overwhelmed with relief to find the dog alive and sitting up.

"Does that mean she's going to be okay?"

Dr. Cook kneeled beside Robin and considered. "If she'd been badly injured internally, she wouldn't have come out of shock, so I'd say her chances are good now. The leg was a good clean break, so that'll be no problem." He scratched his nose absentmindedly and frowned.

"That leg should be pinned today, though. This is a heck of a time for my wife to get the mumps! I have to have somebody to hand me things while I operate, and she usually helps." There was a long pause. "Do you think you could give me a hand?"

Robin swallowed. She hated anything the least bit bloody or painful, and she had fainted the time she'd stepped on a broken milk bottle and had to have stitches in her foot.

The dog inched farther back into the cage. An involuntary yelp of pain escaped her when the leg moved. She was watching the two people warily, expecting them to hurt her more.

Robin winced at the pain in the dog's eyes. "Sure, I'll help. What are you going to do?"

"We're going to pin the bone. Come here; I'll show you." He led the way back to the examining room, which today would serve as operating room, and held up the X rays they had taken yesterday. Against the shadowy black background, the two leg bones, large and small, stood out, clearly showing the jagged break that crossed them both.

He opened a drawer and brought out a long slim plastic package. Sealed inside was a sterile steel rod about the size and shape of a pencil, pointed on each end.

"This is an intermedullary pin. We'll insert it through the wrist joint here"—he pointed to the X ray—"and run it up through the marrow of the bone. That'll hold the bone in place while it heals, and take the pressure off the break, so she'll be able to move around on that leg while it's mending. Then in five or six weeks, when the fracture is healed, we'll go in again and remove the pin. Simple, huh?"

It made Robin shudder to think about it, but she asked, "What about the other bone, the little one in back?"

"With the humerus held in place by the pin, the little one will align itself and heal without help. There's no pressure on it, to speak of. We'll keep a splint on the leg for a while, so it doesn't twist when she starts walking on it."

"What will I have to . . ." Robin's voice trailed off.

"Just open packages and hand me things mostly. I'll be in sterile gloves, so I won't be able to touch anything. You'll do okay. The dog will be completely anesthetized, so there won't be any pain involved."

Robin's teeth clenched as she followed him back to the cage, where their patient was still huddled in a far corner. Dr. Cook opened the cage door and stood back a little, urging the dog in a quiet voice to come out. She stiffened and pressed against the back of the cage.

"She's so scared." Robin wanted to cry for her.

"I'd say she's been through a bad time, and not just the accident. Goldens are usually a very friendly, outgoing breed." Dr. Cook cut a strip of gauze from a roller on the wall and tied a large loop in the middle of it. Then, approaching the cage slowly, talking in a soft voice, he reached in and let the loop close around the yellow muzzle. He wrapped it around once, not tight enough to be uncomfortable, then brought the ends under the dog's ears and tied them behind her head. Finally, he reached behind her and slid her out. The dog trembled violently but didn't struggle as she was carried into the operating room and laid on the gleaming steel table.

Robin stood behind her head, moving her hands in the soft folds of the dog's throat and murmuring reassurances while Dr. Cook injected something into the vein of the animal's good front leg. In just a few seconds Robin could feel the cords in the furry neck go slack, and the yellow head relaxed on the table.

29

Dr. Cook bustled around the room, assembling everything he would need, breaking open a sealed packet of sterilized instruments. It was suddenly very hot in the room, and Robin wished desperately that she were out of this white-walled cell. But there was nobody else who could help, and the leg had to be set. The dog needed her.

Dr. Cook tied himself into a sterile green gown, pulled on thin rubber gloves, and came around to stand by the dog's head.

"Dig your thumbnail in between the pads of her foot. See if she moves."

Robin dug. The dog didn't move.

"Good. She's clear under, then," he said. "How do you feel?"

Robin's head snapped up. "Fine. I feel fine."

"Good. I don't want any fainting assistants cluttering up my operating room floor." As he talked, he began to make a tiny incision over the dog's paw. Robin looked quickly out the window. There was a tree outside, with a deserted bird's nest in it, and she kept her eyes glued to the nest.

"Hand me the pin over there, will you. You'll have to open the package for me."

She tore the plastic end off and held the package out for him to take the pin. Inadvertently she looked at the incision he had made. It was small and neat and not gory at all. She dropped the empty package into the wastebasket in the corner and moved around the room, reading the diplomas on the wall and study-ing a chart that showed all the breeds of dogs.

"What grade are you in at school?" asked Dr. Cook.

"Freshman."

"Do you like it?"

"It's okay, I guess." People were always asking if you liked school, and what could you say? *No, I don't care for it much because I have to give speeches in front of the class and nobody asks me to dance and I'm not one of the popular ones?*

It was warm and close in the small room. Dr. Cook, having given up on conversation to take Robin's mind off what he was doing, resorted to humming. He was perspiring freely now, and big drops gathered in his eyebrows and on the tip of his nose. His wife would have patted them off with a Kleenex, but the girl was so white and trying so hard not to look at the dog on the table that he didn't have the heart to ask her to come that close.

Robin was staring at the bird's nest again. There was a hot, buzzing sensation at the back of her neck, and the room kept slipping out of focus. It was the same feeling she'd had when she stepped on the broken bottle. *I just can't faint now,* she told her-self, clenching her jaw. *It would be too awful.*

"Robin, would you get me a tube of suture there on the shelf. In the small green box, second from the right."

She made herself walk past the inert form on the

table to the cluttered shelf beyond. Small box, second from the right. She took off the lid and held the tube out to Dr. Cook, while he removed a length of suture with his forceps. The buzzing in her head was subsiding a little now, and she thought she might make it. She was even able to watch while he closed the buttonhole incision with a small curved needle clamped firmly in a forceps. A neat stitch, then another and another. One final one, and the job was done.

"There we are." With a satisfied grunt, Dr. Cook rolled off the rubber gloves and mopped his face on his sleeve. He raised a window, letting in a reviving waft of fresh air, and Robin breathed easier. While he set about making a splint, Robin picked up the opened packet of instruments and carried them to the counter.

"You can wash those off in cold water if you want," he said.

She took the instruments one by one—knives with tiny blades, and forceps and tweezers and other things she couldn't identify—and held them under the cold running water, rubbing each one carefully with her thumb to get off every little spatter of blood. Then she dried them on a rolling towel and laid them out on the counter.

By that time Dr. Cook was finished with the splint. Robin held the door open for him as he carried the dog back to her cage. He laid the limp form down and carefully placed the leg in a comfortable position.

"How soon will she wake up?" Robin looked over his shoulder at the big golden dog.

"Oh, she'll be awake but groggy by tonight. I'll come out after supper and give her water. She's going to be thirsty as the dickens after that anesthesia. By tomorrow morning she'll be pretty much herself."

"Will it be okay if I stop in for a minute on my way to school, to see her?"

Robin looked so serious, so motherly, that Dr. Cook couldn't help smiling. "She'd be disappointed if you didn't. And by the way, thanks very much for helping in there today. I don't know what I'd have done without you to give me a hand. A lot of people wouldn't have been able to do it."

Her face lit up at the praise, and she blushed and grinned. "You're welcome. I enjoyed it. It was interesting. Well, see you in the morning, then." And she left for home.

FOUR

Robin left the house a half hour earlier than usual Monday morning to give herself plenty of time to visit the dog. She found Dr. Cook already at work, hosing down the runs behind the building. He turned off the hose when he saw Robin on the other side of the fence, and let her in the back door.

"I moved our patient over to a big cage this morning, so she can have an outdoor run. She'll need to exercise that leg." He motioned to the last of the row of pens.

Robin went to the gate and looked in. The dog was crouched in the corner, watching Robin with suspicious eyes. She looked much better this morning.

The mud had been brushed out of her coat, and she looked a shade less gaunt than she had before, and somehow bigger.

"Hi, brown eyes," Robin said softly. The dog didn't respond. "Come here and let me pet you. I'm not going to hurt you. Come on." The dog huddled farther in the corner.

"She's had a bad time of it," Dr. Cook said, behind Robin. "We don't know what kind of treatment she might have had before the accident. She may have good reason not to trust us very much."

Robin looked at the fear in the dog's eyes, and her heart went out to the animal. "How long will you want to keep her here, Dr. Cook?"

"Oh, I'd like to have her till the end of the week anyway. She'll have to be kept pretty quiet till then, and I want to keep an eye on that leg."

The end of the week. Robin wanted to ask how much the bill was going to be, but she was afraid to find out. Even so, looking at the big yellow dog who watched her so fearfully, Robin began to hope against hope that she wasn't claimed.

The day dragged. Almost before the sound of the dismissal bell had died away, Robin was out the door of the school and heading toward downtown as fast as her straight skirt would let her walk. She passed the drugstore where the other kids were beginning to gather, hardly even noticing that Dwight Wolber was there with Judy Braithewaite.

Robin had more important things to do today.

She pushed through the door of the *Cedar Grove Weekly Messenger*, the town's only newspaper, and gave her lost-and-found ad to the woman behind the counter. "A dollar twenty," the woman said, counting the words. Robin laid down the money and left. The paper wouldn't come out till Wednesday, so she'd just have to be patient till then.

After leaving the newspaper office, she headed back up Maple, past her house and on to the clinic. Maybe her dog had gotten worse during the day. But when she got there, the retriever was in the same corner she had been in that morning.

Robin leaned over the gate and began talking to her, trying to coax her over. Dr. Cook came into the back room then, with a stack of pans filled with dog food. He handed one to Robin and said, "Here, why don't you take this in to her. She ought to be pretty hungry by now."

Taking the pan, Robin opened the gate and stepped into the pen. She set the pan down in the far corner, opposite the dog but not too close. Then she backed up and sat down on the floor of the pen, on the theory that the dog might be less afraid of her on that level.

The dog looked from Robin to the food and back again, but didn't move. Robin talked softly to her for a long time, saying anything that came into her head. When she couldn't think of anything more to say, she began to sing, again very softly. She sang the school song and all the popular ones she could think of, then started on the old ones she'd sung at church camp last summer.

"K-K-K-Katy, beautiful Katy," she sang. "You're the only g-g-g-girl that I adore. . . ." For the first time the dog responded, raising her head a little.

"Oh, you like that one, huh? Okay, I'll sing it again. K-K-K-Katy, beautiful Katy . . ." This time the dog definitely raised her head. Robin wasn't sure, but she thought the tip of the dog's tail might have moved just a fraction.

"Is that your name, girl? Katy? Nice Katy. I think I'll call you that whether it is or not. You have to have a name, don't you, Katy?"

Robin sat there a long time, talking but making no move toward the dog. At last she stood up and backed out of the pen, calling a soft good-bye to Kate. At the back door of the clinic, she turned. The dog was standing over the dish of food now, her eyes still following Robin warily.

The *Weekly Messenger* was delivered about suppertime on Wednesday night. Robin met the delivery boy on the front steps and took the paper from him, turning quickly to the classified ads. There was an ad for lost eyeglasses, one for a found billfold, and one for a found female golden retriever, vicinity of McNeal Park, call Robin Morgan at 633-7719.

"Darn," Robin muttered. "They got the phone number right."

She didn't taste a bite of her supper. The telephone sat on a small stand in the corner of the dining room, and at any minute it could shrill, and someone could say, "You found my dog." She ate enough supper to satisfy her mother and then sat pushing her food around with her fork until it was time to start doing the dishes. She had just begun carrying plates into the kitchen when the phone rang. Heart pounding, Robin stopped in the middle of the kitchen, dropping a knife off the stack of plates in her hands. She didn't even hear it clatter to the floor.

Her father answered the phone. "Hello. . . . Yes, just a minute. Addy, for you. Mrs. Parrish."

Robin breathed again and set the dishes on the counter. A little later the phone rang again. Again Mr. Morgan answered it. This time he called for Robin. She wiped the soapsuds off her hands onto a dish towel and walked slowly into the dining room.

"Hello?"

"Hi, Rob. Darlene. Listen, have you started on your algebra yet? I can't even figure out what we're supposed to be doing with these darn problems."

It was a long evening. Robin spread her homework over the dining room table and sat where she could watch the kitchen clock as she worked. With every half hour, her hopes rose. Surely if Kate's owner was looking for her, he'd have seen the ad by now, and called. By eight-thirty she was optimistic, and by nine-fifteen she was almost relaxed. Surely no one would dare call this late.

Then the phone rang again. This time Robin answered it.

"Lemme talk to Ralph," a rough voice said.

"I'm sorry; you have the wrong number."

The man growled and hung up, and Robin finished her algebra with a high heart. It looked as if she had herself a dog.

Every day that week Robin ran from school to the clinic, greeted Dr. Cook, and went to sit on the floor of Kate's pen. After the first day, she brought her books from school and read her assignments aloud. And always Dr. Cook saved Kate's dinner for Robin to give her.

The second day was like the first. Kate huddled in her corner, never taking her eyes off Robin and making no move toward the food until Robin left. On Wednesday, while Robin read to her, Kate relaxed enough to lower herself until she was lying against the back wall, her head pillowed on the splint. She still watched Robin constantly, but a little of the suspicion left her eyes. Robin was wise enough to make no move toward the dog except with her voice.

On Thursday afternoon, when Robin appeared outside the pen, Kate's tail quivered. It wasn't quite a wag, but Robin saw it, and she was flooded with such a rush of warmth it was all she could do to keep from touching the dog. As she read, she interspersed the dry paragraphs with "How about that, Katy?" "Isn't that right, Katy?" "Good old Katy." At each mention of the name, the tail quivered again.

On Friday afternoon, Robin had read less than a page when she saw Kate stand and take a slow step toward the dish of dog food in the corner. The dog's eyes never left Robin, and she was ready to cringe back into her corner at the slightest move from the girl. Robin read on, carefully keeping the excitement out of her voice. Kate took another step, then lowered her head, still watching Robin, and snatched a mouthful of food. As she bolted the bite, she backed up until she was sitting in her corner again.

But no one had yelled at her. No rough hands had grabbed her neck and forced her head into the food. This quiet girl who came every day and sat talking to her in that gentle voice, saying her name and not grabbing at her, was like no other human being Kate had known. Boldly, she moved again toward the dish, and this time she stood over it until the food was gone. Then she lay down again, but not quite so close to the wall.

Robin, her heart thumping, let one hand drop to the floor. It lay there, just a foot from Kate's nose. It was awkward to turn the pages, but she left her hand there, and after an endless time the yellow head began to inch toward it.

Kate's nose felt rough and dry when it finally brushed Robin's fingers. Robin felt the dog's warm moist breath in her palm. She kept reading, her voice barely above a whisper. Then Kate's muzzle was lying across her hand, and very gently she began to rub the dog's throat with her fingertips.

For the first time in her memory, Kate was experiencing a caress, and it unleashed emotions in the dog that were new and powerful. She wanted to be closer to the girl, but it still might be a trick.

Robin's hand moved gradually down the dog's throat until she was rubbing the bony chest, her fingers touching the top of the splint. Kate crawled a little closer, then closer still, until at last she was sitting in the crook of Robin's arm and the girl's hand was stroking her side. Her tail trembled against the floor as she reached out and licked the girl's cheek. It was wet and salty.

Robin stayed with her dog that day until she heard Dr. Cook locking the front door of the clinic. Then very slowly she stood up, whispered good-bye to Kate, and backed out of the pen.

She found Dr. Cook at the reception desk, counting up the day's receipts. "When do you think Kate can go home?" she asked hopefully.

He finished the column of figures he was adding, then straightened up. "Oh, you could take her tomorrow if you want. I'll have to change the splint in a week or so, but then she won't need anything till time to take out the pin."

"How—um—how much will the bill come to?" She gripped the edge of the counter.

"Well now, let's see here." Dr. Cook consulted the list of prices taped on the inside of the counter over the desk. Intermed. pinning, twenty-five dollars; four X rays at three dollars each; penicillin three times at two dollars a shot; plus seven days' board at a dollar a day would come to . . . fifty dollars. He looked up. Robin was watching him tensely. "Ah, thirty dollars, all told. But your credit is good."

Robin eased her grip on the counter. Thirty dollars wasn't as bad as she'd expected. But it was still a lot more than she had, and she'd be darned if she'd ask her folks for it.

"I've got eight dollars of it," she said. "My allowance is a dollar a week, and I think I can get at least one baby-sitting job a week. That's usually about two dollars."

"Well, yes, that would be okay." He paused and studied the earnest brown-eyed girl. "Or—I had been thinking about getting some part-time help, Saturday afternoons. My wife has her hands full with the house and the kids and helping me during the week. You did such a good job with the bone pinning. Do you think you'd be interested in something like that?"

Would she be interested! "Sure, I'd be interested, but do you really think I could . . . handle it all right?

I've never had any kind of a job. And to be real honest, I almost fainted last Sunday when you were operating."

He laughed and resisted an impulse to pat her head. "Of course you can handle it. If I didn't think so, I wouldn't have suggested it. And I *did* faint at my first operation, at school. Don't tell my wife; she thinks I'm a pillar of strength."

There was a pause, each waiting for the other to speak. Finally, Robin said, "Well, if you really think I could, I'd love to try."

"Fine, fine. How about every Saturday, from noon to five, and you can start tomorrow if you like. Dollar fifty an hour all right? That would be seven fifty a week, and you can apply as much as you like toward the bill. In fact"—he frowned thoughtfully—"if you like the work, and do a good job, maybe we can work out something for this summer."

Robin could only smile foolishly at him, her eyes shining.

FIVE

Robin wasn't sure how her folks were going to feel about the job, but when she told them at supper that night, they were delighted.

"I think it'll be good for you, dear," her mother said. "And you'll have some extra money for school clothes now. I'll tell you what—from now till the end of school, you're excused from Saturday housecleaning. You'll need some time to take care of your dog."

"Which reminds me," her father joined in. "When are you bringing the dog home?"

"Tomorrow, after work." Robin savored the sound of "after work."

"That soon?" His gray eyebrows went up. "Then

we'd best be getting to work on Cindy's pen. I was looking at it today, and the fence is still pretty good. One post is down, and the gate needs a new latch, but it shouldn't take long to get it fixed up." He drained his coffee cup and smiled over it at his daughter. "If you're through eating, we can get some of it done before dark."

Robin looked from him to her mother. They really weren't half bad when the chips were down.

She was up early the next morning, rifling through her closet. What did a veterinarian's assistant, or whatever she was, wear? He hadn't told her what her duties would be. If she wore a skirt and blouse, maybe she'd end up cleaning pens. Or if she wore slacks, maybe she'd be stationed in the reception room, meeting the public. She could run over there and ask him this morning, but it seemed like something she ought to know without having to ask.

She skipped breakfast and had an early lunch, in order to give herself plenty of time to be there by noon. In fact she arrived at the clinic ten minutes early, dressed in a blouse and skirt, and her best flat shoes.

A woman stood in the reception room with a Pomeranian in her arms. She was listening respectfully while Dr. Cook gave her instructions.

He stood behind the counter, one foot on the desk chair, tapping a tiny bottle of pills with his pencil.

". . . in the morning; don't feed him the night before, but he can have water or milk if he wants. Bring him back in two weeks, and we'll check him again. Hi, Robin."

Robin smiled and stood against the wall till the woman left.

"All ready to go to work, assistant?"

She nodded.

"That's good, because I'm starving. I'm going up to the house for lunch now. If anyone wants me, I'll be back at one. Just poke around here all you want, find out where things are, and catch the phone. If you need me, this button on the phone will buzz me at the house. Okay? Okay. See you in an hour."

It felt strange to be left alone in the clinic. In charge. She, Robin Louise Morgan, in charge of things. It was a heady feeling, and a little frightening. She was glad Dr. Cook would be just next door. She set her purse under the desk and went to see Kate.

The dog was standing in the middle of her pen. From habit, she scurried to the far corner when the door opened, but Robin squatted just inside the pen, extending her hand cautiously and talking to the dog. In a few minutes Kate took a step toward her, then another and Robin was rubbing her ears. Kate moved even closer, the tip of her tail quivering tensely. Robin wanted very much to stay with her dog, but she was on duty now, and somebody might come in up front.

She left Kate and wandered back to the reception room, looking in doors along the hallway as she went. There were only four main rooms: the reception room across the front, the small examining room behind it, and a combination office and laboratory across the hall from the examining room. Behind these was a tiny darkroom for developing X rays, and a small storage closet, then the large work and kennel room at the back. The clinic was neat, compact, and pleasantly clean and light, with a minty disinfectant smell. Robin had a feeling she was going to enjoy working there.

She sat at the reception desk, opening drawers and examining the miniature file cabinet that held a card for each of Dr. Cook's patients. There was a ledger on the desk, opened to a page marked "Saturday, April 24." The entries so far were: "Johnson, Bob, board 3 days, $3.00 pd; Eckles, Ruth, worm caps, $2.00, chg." This is easy enough to figure out, Robin thought. At the back of the book she found places for entering expenses, rent, utilities, wages, and another section to list money taken in. She hoped Dr. Cook would trust her to do the bookkeeping this summer, if he kept her on.

The phone rang once, and Robin answered gravely, "Dr. Cook's office." It was a Mrs. Goldberg, wanting to bring her cat in for a rabies shot. Any time after one o'clock, Robin told her, hoping that was the right thing to say. When the woman had hung up, Robin looked through the file drawer till she found the card marked "Goldberg, S. J., cat— Timothy." She laid the card out on the desk and attached a note saying "Rabies shot, sometime after one."

A little before one a man came in, leading a German shepherd with a bandaged ear. Robin put on what she hoped was a professional smile and gripped the edge of the desk.

"Can I help you?"

"Doctor in? He wanted to look at Hans's ear today."

Robin glanced at the clock and wondered if she should buzz Dr. Cook. It was nearly one o'clock, though, so she said, "He's out to lunch, but he'll be right back. Would you care to wait?"

The man dropped heavily into a chair, and Hans stretched out at his feet. "We'll wait. If I go home, the old lady'll make me mow the yard."

Robin smiled and wished she had something to do to look busy. She could get out the man's card anyway. She asked his name, found the card, and laid it on top of Mrs. Goldberg's.

Then Dr. Cook was back, buttoning himself into a clean white jacket and holding open the door to the examining room for Hans and his master. He came around by Robin, started to open the file drawer, then saw the man's card lying on the desk. He glanced quickly at Robin as he picked up the card and said,

"You catch on fast, Nurse Nelly."

She hardly had time to savor the compliment before the door opened again to admit a young housewife in bright orange slacks, carrying a cardboard box full of tiny cocker spaniel puppies that needed their tails docked. She had never been in the clinic before, she said, so Robin searched the desk till she found the blank file cards, then filled in the required information. The woman sat down with her box balanced on her lap, and another woman, a large, well-dressed matron, came in with a huge black cat under her arm.

"I'm Mrs. Goldberg," she announced. "I called about Timmie's rabies shot."

"Oh yes. It'll just be a few minutes. Won't you sit down? He's a beautiful cat."

The woman looked pleased. "Yes, he's our itty-bitty Timmie." She rubbed her sagging chin on the cat's head and looked as though she might purr herself. Robin smiled warmly at Timothy and hoped she'd never act that silly over a cat. In public anyway.

For the next two hours a procession of pet-bearing people moved through the clinic, and Robin was kept busy taking their names, finding their cards, and remembering who had come in first. After each patient, Dr. Cook dropped the card on the desk in front of Robin, with the charges marked on it, then took the next patient's card and left her to collect the money.

By midafternoon, there was a lull, and Robin was

able to catch her breath. She was leafing through the stack of cards accumulated during the day when a girl who looked about Robin's age came through the door, pushing it open with her hips because she was carrying three opened bottles of pop.

"Can I help you?" Robin asked automatically.

"No, but you can help yourself. Coke or orange? Oh, I'm sorry," the girl said, meeting Robin's surprised look. "I forgot to introduce myself. I'm Jan Cook. Coke or orange?"

"Oh. How do you do," Robin said foolishly. "Coke, I guess. Thank you."

Dr. Cook pushed through the door from the lab. "Did I hear somebody offering free refreshments out here? Hi, Charlie." He swatted his wife playfully on the rear of her shorts and took the bottle of orange. "Have you women introduced yourselves? Come on back in the office where we can relax awhile, you two."

They took their dripping cold bottles into the office and sat down, Jan on the corner of her husband's small metal desk.

She took a long pull on her bottle and looked over it at Robin. "Well, how do you like the work so far?"

"So far I love it," Robin said earnestly. "I don't really know what I'm doing yet, but I think it'll be fun."

"I'm sorry I didn't have time to show you what to do before the rush was on," Dr. Cook apologized. "You just sort of got hit over the head with it. But

I guess you figured out about the cards and the ledger. Your main job is to keep things moving smoothly up front, keep people happy while they wait. You know, visit with them, fuss over their pets, call them by name when you can."

He tipped back dangerously in his chair, rubber-soled shoes on the desk. "When you've been here awhile, you'll get acquainted with the regulars. Then if you want to go ahead and work this summer like we talked about, and I hope you will 'cause I think you're a good little worker, I'll show you some of the lab procedures, and X ray developing, and the bookkeeping."

Robin's eyes shone. "I'd like that."

"Hallelujah!" Jan raised her Coke bottle in salute. "A whole summer with nothing to do but keep house and chase the little monsters. I'm glad you came along, Robin." She grinned, and Robin decided she was going to like Mrs. Cook.

It was hard to think of her as Mrs. Cook, though. She looked about sixteen, with her black hair pulled back in a ponytail, and no makeup. Not that she needed makeup. Robin compared herself with the woman on the desk and sighed. Then the front door opened, and the rush was on again.

Five o'clock came surprisingly fast. Dr. Cook locked the front door and showed Robin how to add up the day's receipts on the ledger and check them against the money in the cash box in the top drawer of the desk. Luckily, it checked out to the penny.

At a few minutes after five, the Morgans' car pulled up in front of the clinic, as Robin had asked, and Mrs. Morgan waved through the window to let Robin know she was there.

When the money was counted and the drawer locked, Dr. Cook went to the back room with Robin to get Kate. They both had doubts about how the dog was going to react to leaving the safety of her pen.

"Hi, Katy. Ready to go home?" Robin crooned over the pen door. Wadding Cindy's old leash in her hand, she stepped inside and squatted, holding out her hand so that Kate could smell the leash. The dog stiffened at the sight of it, but took a hesitant step forward, sniffed it, and allowed Robin to rub it against her neck.

Kate had no collar, so Robin very slowly wrapped the leash around her neck, threading the snap end through the loop end and drawing it up around the yellow ruff. Again Kate tensed, then relaxed. Robin backed out of the pen, holding the door open and pulling just the slightest bit on the leash. Kate took a slow, hobbling step, then another and she was out in the room. Robin sighed. Kate was going to be okay.

Robin led the dog out the back door and around the side of the building, matching her stride to Kate's humping walk. Everything went smoothly until they rounded the corner of the building. Then Kate saw the car and pulled back so violently that Robin nearly lost her hold on the lead. Yelping pitifully, Kate tried to scramble back around the corner, out of sight of the car. Afraid she might hurt her leg, Robin led the dog back around the clinic. Dr. Cook was just coming out the back door.

"What happened? I heard her yelping like the devil was after her."

"She was scared of the car. I guess because of the accident. Now how am I going to get her home? She can't walk that far." Robin was disgustingly near to tears.

"Hmmm." He pinched his lips. "I know." He went into the building and came back with a wheelbarrow. "I'll push, and you can walk beside it to keep her from jumping out."

Robin led Kate all around the wheelbarrow for a good look at it. Then, when the dog was reassured, Dr. Cook lifted her and placed her inside. Kate flattened herself against the bottom, but made no move to jump out. They started down the sidewalk, Dr. Cook pushing the wheelbarrow, Kate riding like a timid furry sultan, and Robin walking close beside, holding the leash and keeping a steadying hand on Kate's neck. Mrs. Morgan drove slowly behind them and hoped no one would recognize her.

At the corner of Fourth Avenue they stopped to let a car go by before easing the wheelbarrow down over the curb. Robin glanced up as the car slowed for the intersection and met the surprised stare of

Dwight Wolber. Judy Braithewaite was in the car with him, and a couple of the other kids in that crowd were in the back seat. They all stared blankly at Robin before they waved. She stared right back at them. So what if they thought she was nuts! Kate was more important than those stuck-up kids, anyway. But Robin's face burned, and it was a relief when they drove on.

At last the journey was accomplished, and Kate was lifted out and set down in the pen beside the Morgans' garage. She stood where she was until Robin slipped off the leash and closed the gate and Dr. Cook and the wheelbarrow left. Then, while Robin sat down on a tree stump to watch her new dog, Kate limped about the enclosure, sniffing through the weedy grass.

"Come here, Katy; here, girl." Kate wagged her tail faintly in apology, but stood where she was. Her confidence in Robin had been shaken by the ride and the new surroundings. Regretfully, Robin left the dog and went up to the house. She noticed that her mother had parked the car in the street rather than driving past the pen to put it in the garage, and she was grateful for that thoughtfulness.

After supper the whole family went out to see the dog, and to bring her food and water. Kate stood against the back fence and refused to come over to them.

"She's sure a shy thing, isn't she?" Mrs. Morgan observed.

"She was scared of the car because one hit her." Robin came to Kate's defense. "And I think somebody was mean to her before that. Dr. Cook says golden retrievers are usually very friendly. And she likes me."

Robin's father only commented on how thin the dog was.

"She doesn't have to stay out here all night alone, does she, Mother?" Robin pleaded.

"Now I suppose you want her in your room with you."

"Well, she'll be scared out here in a strange place —her first night, especially." Robin was on the defensive again.

"How about a compromise?" said Mrs. Morgan, smiling. "You can sleep on the cot on the sun porch tonight, and Kate can stay in there with you. But leave her out here till bedtime."

Robin stayed in the pen all evening with her dog, and when it was late enough to go to bed, she led Kate into the sun porch. It was screened in, and Robin had often slept there on hot nights when she was younger. She called for her mother to bring out her pajamas so she wouldn't have to leave Kate alone. Then, still talking constantly to the dog, she got ready for bed and turned out the light.

Her arm hung over the edge of the narrow cot, and in a little while she felt a brush of warm fur and heard a sigh and a light thud, as Kate stretched out on the floor beside the bed. Robin went to sleep finally, smiling, her hand riding lightly on Kate's ribs.

SIX

During the first week of her life at the big yellow house on Maple Street, Kate spent most of her time huddled in a corner of the pen by the garage. Only when Robin came home from school to sit on the stump and talk to her did she come out, taking cautious steps toward the girl, her tail wagging in nervous little jerks, ready to retreat if Robin made a sudden move or a loud noise.

Robin resumed the habit of doing her homework aloud to Kate. She brought an orange crate from the basement to work on, steadying it with her knees when it rocked on the lumpy ground. It wasn't the easiest way to do homework, but Robin wanted to be with Kate every minute she could.

By the end of the first week, as soon as Robin was settled with her books and orange crate, Kate would begin to circle the pen, close to the fence, working her way a little closer to the girl with each turn, stopping often to see if Robin was going to grab at her. The circles would grow smaller until Kate finally stopped beside Robin, her eyes on a level with the top of the crate.

Then, casually, not looking up from her book, Robin would drop her hand, brushing the dog's ear or shoulder. Soon the hand was rubbing under Kate's ears, and the dog would sit down beside the stump, her splint scratching Robin's bare leg, her eyes closed to savor this delicious new feeling of being petted. When the routine reached this stage, Robin was too proud and happy to study.

By the end of the second week, Kate was meeting Robin at the gate, and as long as Robin made no sudden moves, she didn't pull back. But the appearance of anyone else, even Robin's parents, still sent her scurrying for her corner.

Robin invested some of her salary in a round leather collar for Kate and an identification tag. She wasn't taking any chances on the dog's getting lost again.

As soon as she felt that Kate trusted her enough, she began brushing her every day with Cindy's old brush. Kate seemed to enjoy it, because she would lean into the brush with every stroke. She was more relaxed then than at any other time, and often Robin brushed long after she needed to.

Gradually Kate's ribs and hip bones disappeared under a covering of muscle, and her dull, dry yellow coat—thanks to the daily brushing and the sample vitamins that Dr. Cook sent home with Robin—turned into rich golden waves that crackled under Robin's brush. Even Mr. Morgan admitted now that Kate was a pretty thing.

Suddenly, amazingly, it was the first week of June, and the last week of school. Robin had been so engrossed in gaining Kate's confidence and in learning her job at Dr. Cook's that school had become something to be gotten through till she could get back to important things, like her dog. She was too conscientious to let her assignments slide, although she wasn't quite so attentive in class as she had been. But the social aspect of school, the going-withs and the breaking-ups and the crushes, went on around her unnoticed. Dwight Wolber still ignored her as hard as ever, but she didn't really notice; or if she did, it didn't matter too much now. She had Kate, and Kate needed her.

Finally it was all over—the last test and the last assembly, the final cleaning out of desks and lockers, and the last picking up of report cards. Robin got three B's, one A, and one C, but the C was in physical education, so it didn't really count. It was about the same kind of report card she had always brought home.

And then it was summer vacation. Her new hours at the clinic were from noon to five, Tuesday through Saturday, since Saturday was a busy day and Monday wasn't.

The Saturday after school was out, Kate had the pin removed from her leg. Robin brought her to work that noon, and as soon as Dr. Cook was back from lunch, he got out the sterile packs and began preparing for the surgery.

"Are you sure you want to help with this one?" he asked, quirking an eyebrow at Robin. "I can call Jan if you'd rather not."

"I can do it," she said. In the six Saturdays she had worked, she had helped with a tonsillectomy and the removal of an injured eye. She was secretly very proud of the fact that, aside from a kind of queasy stomach during the eye removal, she hadn't even come close to fainting again. And she was getting so she could clean up the room and the instruments afterward with complete professional detachment. If anybody was going to assist with Kate, it would be Robin herself.

"Have it your way, Nurse Nelly." Dr. Cook grinned. "This won't take very long anyway. I'll just have to reopen the incision over the joint, go in with this special forceps, and pull out the pin. If I do say so myself, we got a beautiful mend." Earlier in the month they had taken another set of X rays to be sure the bones were in proper alignment and the pin was still in place.

Kate was brought in, injected with the anesthetic, and the work began. Robin, determined to see it through, stood by Kate's head and forced herself to watch as the blade parted a layer of skin, then a layer of muscle. Then the floor was moving under Robin's feet, the walls were wavering, and her ears were roaring so loudly she could barely hear Dr. Cook say sharply, "Go outside and sit with your head down."

With a tremendous effort, she moved toward the door to the reception room, opening it clumsily and aiming herself at the front door. If she could just make it out to the fresh air . . . But someone was coming in. A figure was standing in front of her, holding something out and speaking. Her head cleared a little, and the roar in her ears subsided to a buzz. Her eyes were able to focus on the woman in front of her.

"I'm sorry; what did you say?" Robin blushed and felt foolish.

The woman held out a small brown dachshund and repeated, "I said I have a boarder for you. This is Gretchen. I called yesterday to make a reservation. We're going to see the grandchildren in California."

"Oh, yes." Robin was nearly herself again. "You're Mrs. . . ."

"Ethridge. We haven't seen our daughter since

the last baby came, and the oldest is almost five now. Nobody believes I look old enough to have a five-year-old grandson."

Robin smiled politely and got out the card for Ethridge.

"Be sure and take good care of Gretchy now. Here's her rubber mouse and her blanket, and I'm leaving a handkerchief of mine so she won't get lonesome." The items were piled into Robin's arms. "You'll look in on her during the day, won't you, dear? She's not used to being in a kennel, and I know she'd feel better if you would pay some extra attention to her. Bye-bye, Gretchy-Wetchy. Don't worry; Mommy's coming back just as soon as I can to take you out of this mean old place. Be a good little doggy now." And she left.

Sighing, Robin took Gretchy-Wetchy and her belongings, and put them in a freshly disinfected cage in the back room.

By the time she got back to the operating room, Dr. Cook was just tying off the final stitch on Kate's leg, and the intermedullary pin was in the wastebasket.

"Well, you look a little better than you did a minute ago," Dr. Cook said cheerfully.

Robin blushed, furious with herself for almost passing out.

"Don't feel bad, Nurse Nelly. It was because it was your own dog. Happens all the time. Heaven knows I couldn't operate on Gorgeous. It's all I can do to give him his shots." Gorgeous was the Cooks' huge boxer-collie-sheepdog.

Robin felt a little better then.

Kate's leg healed rapidly after that, and before long the only reminder of the broken bone was a small lump that ringed her leg where the break had mended. It was just a calcium deposit, Dr. Cook assured Robin, a healthy sign, and it would disappear in a month or so.

The dog had the run of the house now. The only time she was shut in her pen was while Robin was at work. She still wasn't making any friendly overtures to Robin's parents, but she didn't back away from them either, and if Mrs. Morgan wanted to scratch Kate's throat while she read or watched television, that was all right with Kate. Now that the splint was off so she could climb stairs easily, she slept every night on the shaggy white rug beside Robin's bed.

The thirty-dollar debt had long since been paid, and now that Robin was working five afternoons a week, the money was piling up in her new savings account. She spent a little of it for a new dish for Kate and a book on golden retrievers, and she splurged on a red-checked shorts and blouse outfit and a full-skirted white sundress with brown embroidery on the puffy sleeves. But most of the money went into the bank. There was still the possibility that Kate's owner would show up, and in that case Robin was prepared to buy her from him, no matter how much it cost.

During the quiet mid-week afternoons, Dr. Cook began teaching Robin some of the things there wasn't time to explain on the hectic Saturdays. He showed her how to work the autoclave that sterilized syringes and surgical instruments, how to bathe dogs and trim toenails and clean ears, how to develop X-ray film in the tiny darkroom, and how to keep the books.

Also, she did her share of floor mopping, dusting, scouring, and disinfecting. And she loved every minute of it, especially when people came in and she remembered their names, and they beamed at being remembered. Or when the phone rang and she knew the answers to the caller's questions. There was still a lot she didn't know, of course, and sometimes she gave the wrong answers, but all in all her confidence in her ability to do the right thing was growing every day. Dr. Cook was quick to point out a spot she had missed in cleaning, or a mistake in the ledger, but he was quicker to praise her when she did things right, or anticipated his needs. Every time he praised her for some little thing, Robin stood a fraction taller.

One afternoon when Dr. Cook was in the house helping Jan move the living room furniture, and Robin was sitting at the reception desk getting the end-of-the-month bills ready to mail out, the door opened and a man came in leading a golden retriever.

The dog looked so much like Kate at first glance that Robin's heart caught in her throat. But it wasn't Kate.

"May I help you?" She smiled automatically at the man. He was very tall and very thin, with a neat gray moustache and a perfectly bald, freckled head. His eyes were so deep-set it was hard to tell what color they were, and he carried himself like a general.

He ignored Robin's question. "You must be Tom's new girl. He told me about you. Said you were a big help to him. I'm Carter Crissman, and this pup needs a health certificate. Sold her to a kennel back east, and I'm putting her on a plane tomorrow. Tom in?"

Carter Crissman . . . that name sounded familiar. Robin buzzed the house, told Dr. Cook that Mr. Crissman was here, and thumbed through the file drawer for his card.

Then she remembered. Carter Crissman was the man Dr. Cook had called the day she'd found Kate. The one who raised golden retrievers, out south of town. She was about to tell him that she had a golden, too, when Dr. Cook came in.

"Tom. Good to see you." Mr. Crissman offered his hand in a gesture that was almost a salute. "Need a health certificate here. Shipping her out of state. Fix us up?"

"You bet, Carter. Bring her on in here." They disappeared into the examining room. When they emerged a few minutes later, Mr. Crissman was carrying a small blue form that stated that the dog had been inoculated against rabies and was free from any apparent disease. The two men stood beside the counter for a while talking, while Robin followed the conversation from her desk.

Then Mr. Crissman said, "What became of that golden you called me about awhile back? Find the owner?"

"No, nobody claimed her. My secretary's got her now." He nodded toward Robin and winked.

"That so?" Mr. Crissman looked at Robin with new interest. "Was she badly hurt?"

"She had a broken leg, but it's all healed now," Robin said. "I was noticing when you came in, this dog looks an awful lot like Kate. To me, anyway," she finished lamely.

"Oh? She could be from my bloodlines. I'd like to take a look at her. I can usually spot a dog of Copper Lane breeding. You know where I live?" Robin nodded. "Bring her out some time. You might enjoy seeing my dogs, too. Thanks, Tom." He waved the blue certificate and left.

"Say, Nurse Nelly, that was a compliment. Carter Crissman doesn't invite just anybody to see his kennel." Dr. Cook grinned at her from under his eyebrows, and Robin glowed.

SEVEN

The next Monday Robin took her courage in hand and started off on the three-mile hike to the Crissman house. Kate was still terrified of cars, and Robin didn't trust her not to run away if she rode her bike, so there was no alternative but to walk. She ate an early lunch and brushed Kate till she shone. Then, snapping the new leash to Kate's collar, she started off toward Highway 68.

The worst of the summer heat hadn't arrived yet, and the breeze was cool, but there was little shade along the highway. They hadn't walked far before Robin was hot and dusty. She kept to the shoulder, as far from the highway as she could get, and stayed between Kate and the cars. At first Kate stopped and shook at every passing car, but it wore off.

Finally a discreet sign appeared, announcing "Copper Lane Golden Retrievers." The house, a neat brick story and a half, sat far back from the highway, flanked by giant pine trees and low pillowy shrubs. Red geraniums lined the flagstone walk and underscored the windows.

Before starting up the drive, Robin took off her steamed and dusty glasses and rubbed the lenses on her shorts. Somehow the formal neatness of the house and lawn made her wish she had dressed up a little more.

She led Kate up the graveled drive to the house, then stood undecided. The house looked empty, so she went around it toward what was obviously the kennel, a long, low white building with fenced runs on either side. She was standing in front of it, wondering whether to go in or to forget the whole thing and bolt for home when Mr. Crissman came around the corner of the kennel, saw her, and waved.

He looked a little less military today, in denim work pants and a plaid cotton shirt. He wiped the palms of his hands against his pants legs, leaving streaks of dirt, and approached.

"Well. This is the dog. Glad you brought her. What was your name again?"

"Robin Morgan, and this is Kate."

Mr. Crissman walked around Kate, who pressed

against Robin's bare leg and watched him suspiciously. He looked at her from every angle, going, "Um-hmm, um-hmm," like a dentist counting cavities. Finally he turned toward the kennel and shouted, "Frank, come out here a minute. Frank's my kennel manager," he explained to Robin. "I want him to take a look at your dog."

Frank appeared, was introduced to Robin, and stood back to study Kate, much as Mr. Crissman had. He was as short and square as his employer was tall and thin. His face was round and pudgy and somehow elfish, and his legs were bowed from supporting his thick, broad-shouldered body. When they were introduced, he smiled at Robin and shook hands gravely, and he spoke softly to Kate while he looked her over.

"What's her breeding?" he asked Robin.

"I don't know. I found her."

Frank looked quickly from Robin to Mr. Crissman. "She looks like a Campaigner pup, don't she, boss?"

"Just what I was thinking." Mr. Crissman walked around Kate again to study her head. "She's got his head. More refined of course. His ear placement. Let's see how she moves. Take her down the drive and back at a fast walk, young lady. Hold her head up."

Robin did as she was told. Kate paced down the drive, pressing close to the girl's legs and tucking her

69

tail between her legs as though the men might take a shot at her from behind. Returning, Kate hung back a little. She had thought she was going home.

Frank squinted up at Mr. Crissman. "I don't know, boss. The dog's so tensed up it's hard to tell what her natural gait looks like. She could be a Campaigner pup."

Robin cleared her throat. "What's a Campaigner pup?"

The two men turned to look at her as though they had forgotten she was there. Mr. Crissman said, "Come inside and I'll show you. You can turn Kate into that end run over there."

She led Kate into the long narrow pen beside the building and turned her loose, carefully latching the gate. Then she followed the men into the kennel. Through an attractive wood-paneled office, hung with photographs of retrievers, they went into the main part of the building, a long, narrow room lined on either side with pens, each with an outside run. The partitions were tan glazed tile on the bottom half, and wire mesh on top. There were narrow troughs in the floor in front of the pens to carry off the water from the daily hosing and scrubbing.

The three moved slowly down the row of pens, stopping before each one to look at the dogs inside, reaching in to ruffle ears or scratch throats. "This is Champion Hildy of Copper Lane," Mr. Crissman said of one dog that was loudly barking welcome to them. "And this is a youngster just coming along." He smiled at the dog in the next pen. "If I haven't sold him by fall, we'll start showing him then."

One pen held a mother and eight surging ten-day-old puppies. At Mr. Crissman's invitation, Robin went into the pen, stroked the mother dog, and touched several of the puppies, none of whom paid any attention to her in their battle for milk. The mother raised her head when Robin came in, beat a happy tattoo on the floor with her tail, and waited for compliments on her babies. Robin sat on the floor and took one of the pups on her lap. His tiny paws swam against her leg, and his heavy head waved and bobbed and bumped at her bare knee. Robin looked over her shoulder at the two men leaning on the gate.

"I thought show dogs were supposed to be high-strung. She doesn't even seem to care if a stranger picks up her puppies."

Mr. Crissman smiled. "Purebred dogs aren't any more nervous than other dogs, and the goldens are a very easygoing breed. There's not a dog in my kennel that any stranger couldn't walk right up to. They all love kids. Not that they see many around here." His voice trailed off almost sadly.

Robin returned the puppy to its family and stood up. On down the line they went. At the last pen, a note of thinly concealed pride crept into Mr. Crissman's voice as he nodded to the dog inside.

"And this is International Champion Copper Lane's Campaigner, top winning golden retriever in the country two years ago. Won Best Sporting Dog at Madison Square Garden and at the Chicago International show the same year. Considered one of the outstanding goldens in America."

During this introduction the dog had jumped up to drape his paws over the top of the gate. Mr. Crissman rumpled his ears roughly and slapped his shoulders, while the dog's tail whipped excitedly and his hind feet danced on the floor in an effort to get closer. Robin stretched out her hand, and the welcome was transferred immediately to her.

In spite of his titles, he looked to Robin pretty much like the other dogs in the kennel. He was a little bigger, and his coat was longer and more profuse, but that was all the difference her untrained eye could see.

She looked up at Mr. Crissman, who was still staring fondly at Campaigner. "Was this the one . . . you said something about Kate. . . ."

Frank, who had been silent till now, said, "We was just saying your little dog looked like she could be a daughter of his. She has his head and his coat."

Apprehension touched Robin. "You mean she might have belonged to you once, Mr. Crissman?"

They left Campaigner peering wistfully over his gate, and started slowly back toward the office. "No, not necessarily, young lady. Campaigner has sired pups for breeders all over the country. Or she could be one that I bred and sold as a puppy."

He held open the office door to let Robin through. "Your Kate is quite timid, isn't she? That's the only thing that makes me wonder if she is a daughter of Cam's. Go get her and bring her in."

The two men, tall and short, leaned against the huge walnut desk in the office while Robin got Kate from the run and brought her inside. They closed the doors and turned her loose; she promptly jumped onto the leather couch beside Robin and pressed close to her side, watching the men.

"She always been that timid?" Frank asked, fishing a dead cigar out of the ashtray and relighting it.

"Since I've had her anyway." Robin told them about finding Kate and about how she had worked with the dog to gain her confidence. "She still won't go near a car," she concluded dismally. After seeing the Crissman dogs, it was hard not to be just a little ashamed of Kate's cringing.

"Hmmm. Well now, there's shyness and shyness in dogs." Mr. Crissman took a deep breath, settled himself more comfortably against the desk, and crossed his arms. "There's shyness that results from unwise line breeding—that is, mating dogs that are too closely related over too many generations. You can get some top dogs with line breeding, but you run the risk of coming up with some undesirable traits. If that's Kate's problem, you might as well get used

73

to it, because she's always going to be like this."

They all looked at Kate, and she trembled and pressed harder against Robin.

"Or," Mr. Crissman continued, "if a basically good-natured dog is badly treated over a long enough time, he may go sour, and understandably so. Then again, a good dog can become kennel shy just from being shut up all his life with no human companionship or attention, even though he's never been actually mistreated. But in that case they usually come out of it in time, given a good home and lots of affection. Kennel shy dogs often make the best pets when they do start to trust you, because they've been wanting that love and not getting it."

Immediately Robin was sorry for having felt ashamed of Kate, even for a minute. "Which kind of shy do you think Kate is?" She looked hopefully from Frank to Mr. Crissman.

Frank rolled the stub of cigar to the other corner of his mouth. "Well now, if she should be a pup of Cam's, it's a safe bet her shyness don't come from her breeding. All his pups as I know of is just as bold as he is, and you saw yourself he ain't no shrinking violet. Course, there's a lot of golden retrievers around, and just 'cause she looks like a Campaigner dog ain't no guarantee she is one."

Mr. Crissman spoke up. "About all you can do is keep working with her, young lady. She's a good golden. Excellent conformation. Got depth and substance. If she was registered in your name so she could be shown, she'd be championship material."

Robin looked at Mr. Crissman quickly. Kate, a show dog? For an instant she wondered what Dwight Wolber would say to that. Robin Morgan, owner of a champion. Her hand tightened on Kate's ruff.

"Do you really think she's that good a dog?" Her eyes sparkled as she looked from one to the other. Both men nodded gravely, Mr. Crissman pursing his lips and Frank rolling his cigar. "But how could I get her . . . what was it you said?"

"Registered to you. Before you show a dog, he has to be registered with the American Kennel Club, and only the owner or his agent can sign an entry blank." Mr. Crissman twisted around to paw through the clutter on the desk, and came up with a pamphlet, which he tossed to Robin.

"Take that home with you if you want. It's put out by the AKC. Lists all the rules of dog shows." He frowned. "There's no way to get her registered in your name, though, unless you can find the owner and get him to sell her to you." He suddenly felt sorry for the girl as the eager look died on her face.

"Tell you what," he suggested. "If you like, I'll check my records and see who I've sold Campaigner daughters to in the past few years. A good many of them have gone to people I see at the shows all the time, so that will eliminate them."

He crossed the room to sit on the couch beside

Kate. Gently but firmly, he took her muzzle and examined her teeth. Her eyes widened, and she pulled back a little, but Robin's hand moving on her neck reassured her. He released her head and ran his hands over her body with professional deftness.

Settling back into the couch, he stretched out his legs and crossed his arms over his stomach. "Offhand I'd say she was no more than two years old. I'll check my records for sales, year before last. If you want, that is."

Robin swallowed and studied the toes of her dusty brown loafers. If she said yes, he might turn up Kate's real owner, and if Kate really was a daughter of an international champion, whatever that was, the owner must have paid a lot for her. And of course he'd want her back. But if she said no, it would sound as though she was trying to keep a dog that wasn't really hers. And Kate would never be a show dog. A champion. It was a hard decision.

"Do whatever you think is best, Mr. Crissman," she said finally, in a voice so low he barely heard her. She stood suddenly, and Kate leaped down to stand against her legs.

"Thanks for showing me your dogs. I enjoyed it very much. We'd better be starting for home now. It was nice meeting you, Frank." She gave each of them a quick, wobbly smile and left, letting Kate pull her jerkily down the drive. She didn't want to start getting teary-eyed in front of them.

76

Mr. Crissman opened the door and called, "Come again any time, young lady." Sighing, he closed the door and turned to Frank.

"Whatcha going to do, boss?"

"I'm going to write a few letters," he muttered. "I have an idea whose dog that is, and I'd like to see the girl get legal title to her."

There was a filing cabinet in the corner; he pulled out a drawer and began rifling through the correspondence folder.

"Frank, you remember a man . . . what the heck was his name? Winter before last he stopped in, looking for good breeding stock. From around Chicago someplace. We sold him a dandy little gal about four months old. I remember I didn't want to sell her, she looked so good at that age. Didn't like this fellow's looks, either. Big loudmouth type."

Frank studied the ceiling. "Oh . . . yeah. I think I know the one. He had his kennel man with him. Didn't like either one of 'em, as I recall."

"Here it is." Mr. Crissman pulled a letter from the file. "Dale Cheevers. That's him. He wrote this— let's see—about six months after he bought the dog. Wanted his money back. Complained she was bad tempered and wouldn't let anyone handle her. I wrote back and said the dog wasn't bad tempered when I sold her, and that was the last I heard from him. If I'd had my wits about me, I'd have bought the dog back then and there."

"Might not be the same dog," Frank offered.

"True, but the more I think about it . . ." He pulled out his yearly record book from the bottom file drawer and began leafing through it, glancing over lists of names and dates.

"Here we are." The entry was written in Carter Crissman's neat hand. "Klondike Kate of Copper Lane, whelped 9-12, Sire—Int. Ch. Copper Lane's Campaigner, Dam—Ch. Copper Lane's Gold Strike. Sold 1-5 to Dale Cheevers, Chicago, Illinois. $300.00, pd."

He sat down at the desk and rolled a piece of Copper Lane stationery into the typewriter. Then he sat for a long time, staring out the window, fingers drumming softly on the keys. Should he, or shouldn't he? Was Dale Cheevers the kind of man who wouldn't let the girl keep her golden if it turned out to be his dog? Even if the girl signed over her allowance to him for the rest of her life, as he knew instinctively Robin would?

"Such a nice youngster," he mused, a little wistful. "If Margaret had lived, we might have had a daughter just like this one." He gave his head a firm shake to clear it of such thoughts, and began to type. If Dale Cheevers gave them any trouble, he'd buy the dog back himself. Give her to the girl in exchange for a litter of puppies. They'd work something out.

EIGHT

Robin lay awake a long time that night. Her visit to the Crissman kennel had set up a whole new string of daydreams that were somehow a relief from her usual ones of being popular and finding a Special Boy. Owning a show dog, that was something else again.

On the long walk home she had nearly convinced herself that she did want Mr. Crissman to find Kate's owner, so she could buy Kate from him and never have to worry about having to give her up. Then she could enter her in a dog show . . . she had read the AKC pamphlet from cover to cover after supper, and by now she was eager to show Kate.

Robin sat cross-legged in the middle of her bed, like a Buddha in rumpled pajamas. She could just see Kate, proud and beautiful, winning Best of Breed, or maybe Best of Show.

Kate began to snore lightly on her rug beside the bed, her feet twitching spasmodically, bringing Robin back to reality. There was still Kate's shyness to cure, even if Robin could get official ownership of her.

She mulled over Mr. Crissman's explanation of inbred shyness and the man-made kind, and somehow she knew that Kate's was the curable type. Look how much better she is now than she was when I got her, Robin reassured herself. She'll let me do anything I want, and she likes Mom, and she's not afraid of Daddy now. Only of strangers. And cars.

But show dogs had to ride in cars, or they couldn't get to the shows. There certainly weren't any dog shows within walking distance of Cedar Grove.

"We're going to have to get down to business on this car foolishness, Katy, my girl," she whispered. The dog's paws quit twitching, but she didn't quite wake up.

The next morning, full of optimistic determination, Robin led Kate down Maple Street toward town. The business district of Cedar Grove, like many small midwestern towns, was built around a square. Maple and Elm streets formed the north and south sides, and Ninth and Tenth avenues the east and west sides of the square. In the center was a park that held the gray stone county courthouse, an ornate bandstand in need of paint, and several large old cedars that managed to shade the whole square.

Robin walked along Maple till she came to a spot between the bank and Brown's Shoe Store. There was a lot of pedestrian traffic here, and shade from Brown's awning, and the ledge under the display window was wide enough to sit on, uncomfortably. She stopped and sat.

Kate, who had been walking nervously between Robin and the stores, ducked behind Robin's legs and sat pressed against the brick front of the shoe store. Her worried eyes followed each person who passed.

When no one was near, Robin talked to Kate in a low voice, afraid of being caught. She felt conspicuous, as though everyone in town must be wondering what she was doing there.

Several people who knew Robin or her family nodded, smiled, and said hello as they passed. A few stopped for a minute to ask how her folks were or to comment on the dog. A friend of Robin's mother reached down toward Kate, who shrank back against the wall. Robin quickly explained that the dog wasn't used to strangers and that she was trying to get her accustomed to people. The woman nodded sympathetically, wished Robin luck, and launched into a story about her daughter-in-law's poodle who was *just* like a person, it was so smart.

The cars that circled the square were forced to go slowly, and since they didn't come too close, they didn't bother Kate. Only when one that was parked at the curb in front of them drove off and another nosed into the parking space did she cringe and whimper. When that happened, passersby turned to look curiously at Robin and Kate. Robin forced herself to return their looks.

When they had been there about an hour and Kate had unwound enough to lie down against the building, still watching alertly, a familiar blue Ford went by. Dwight Wolber, tanned, his hair bleached almost white by the summer sun, lolled behind the wheel. Judy Braithewaite, equally tanned and bleached, sat possessively beside him. They saw Robin and waved. She waved back, her ears burning. It was a free country, and if anybody wanted to stand in front of Brown's Shoe Store, they certainly could. But when Dwight and Judy circled past her again, staring even more curiously, Robin began to feel terribly conspicuous.

But she stood her ground, and eventually the blue Ford left the square. By then it was time to go home and get ready for work.

The next morning Robin again took up her post on the window ledge of the shoe store, with Kate sitting behind her legs watching the passing shoppers. She felt even more foolish today than she had yesterday. Nobody in his right mind stands all morning two days in a row in front of a shoe store with a dog. But it was the only way she could think of to get Kate used to crowds, so she sat it out.

About midmorning a boy she had never seen before walked by. Paying no attention to Robin, he smiled down at Kate and called softly, "Hi, pup," as he passed.

Robin watched him go down the street until he turned into the drugstore on the corner. He was surely high school age, but she knew that he didn't go to Cedar Grove. With less than two hundred kids in the whole high school, you couldn't help knowing everybody. Maybe he just moved here, she mused with quickening interest. Any new boy was interesting, until he turned out to be too young or too old, or in a higher social level, out of her reach.

She watched the drugstore until he came out and headed back toward her. Then she leaned down and began nervously unwinding the leash from Kate's front legs. He was almost to her, but she couldn't make herself look up.

"That's a good-looking dog."

Her head snapped up. He was standing there, a magazine rolled up in one fist, looking down at Kate. "Thank you," she said, her voice coming out tight and unnatural.

He looked about seventeen, with kinky black hair that was soft and clean. His eyes were an indefinite blue-gray-green, and his nose was too big. Robin liked his nose instantly. It saved him from being handsome and thus out of reach. He squatted before Kate, extending his hand for her to smell, and smiled up at Robin. It was an unaffected smile that held no reservations about her appearance.

"She's kind of shy with strangers," Robin explained as Kate shrank back from his outstretched hand.

"I'm not going to hurt you, girl," he crooned. "What's her name?"

Thinking he had said, "What's your name?" she answered, "Robin Morgan. What's yours?"

He looked up in quick confusion. "I meant the dog's." He stood, flushing at the unintended rudeness of the words. "My name is Paul Carlisle. What was yours again?"

Robin blushed furiously. Boy, if there was any way to goof things up, she'd find it. "Robin Morgan. The dog is Kate."

"Oh." He squatted again and held out his closed fist. "I just moved here."

"Welcome to Cedar Grove. I hope you like it here." Her words sounded so corny Robin felt herself go red again. And why on earth did she have to wear this awful blouse and the same shorts she'd been scrounging around in all week! Today of all days . . .

He was still trying to coax Kate to him. "Come on,

84

Katy, old girl. I won't hurt you. I hope I'm not keeping you from anything," he said suddenly, rocking back on his heels to look up at Robin. "I'm a nut for dogs."

"No, no," she assured him quickly. "I was just standing here. I'm trying to get Kate used to people." She found herself telling this stranger about finding Kate and visiting Mr. Crissman's. For the first time in years she was talking to a boy without worrying about what he was thinking of her. She could tell from the way he listened that he was interested.

By the time she had finished, Paul Carlisle had his hand under Kate's ear, rubbing gently, and the dog was inching toward him and twisting her head to bring the itchy spot under his fingertips.

"I think she likes me," he said proudly. Then, having achieved his goal of making friends with the dog, he stood. "Well, nice meeting you—um—Robin. See you around."

As Robin watched, he sauntered down the sidewalk, striking each parking meter a glancing blow with his rolled-up magazine. A half block away he turned, waved to Robin, and angled out into the street. He opened the door of a middle-aged pink and white Chevy, slid in, and drove off around the square.

Good! she thought. He had to be at least sixteen, or he wouldn't be driving. He wasn't too young nor too handsome to be hoped for. Nor so homely as to endanger her social standing, such as it was, if he should ask her for a date. And if he didn't know any other kids yet, she had the inside track, for the time being anyway. The rest of the morning Robin didn't notice whether Kate was improving or not.

There was a small mirror inside the door of the closet in Dr. Cook's office where he hung his white jackets. Robin stood looking into it, her glasses dangling from one hand, a dustrag in the other. She leaned in closer, focusing nearsightedly on her image. Without the glasses, and if she could figure out something to do with her darned hair, she might have half a chance with him.

It was midafternoon, and quiet in the clinic. Dr. Cook had driven to Des Moines for a meeting of the State Veterinary Society, so she was alone. She mumbled to herself, "Maybe if I let my hair grow so I could wear it back, like Judy Braithewaite . . ." She tried holding it back at the nape of her neck, but it wasn't long enough for a twist like Judy's or a ponytail like Mrs. Cook's. She dropped her hand and let the nondescript waves fall back into place.

"Anybody home?"

Robin jumped. Jan Cook came into the office, herding her two sons before her.

"Oh. Hi. I didn't hear you come in." Robin jammed her glasses back on, blushing at being caught at the mirror.

"I got lonesome for adult companionship, so I thought I'd come back and bother you for a while. Tommy, take Brucie in the back room with you, honey, and look at the doggies. But don't open any cages . . . or I'll knock your little heads together," Jan finished under her breath as the boys disappeared. She pushed aside a stack of papers on the desk and sat on it, motioning vaguely from Robin to the chair.

"Don't let me keep you from your work if you have any. But I figured it'd be pretty quiet here today, with the whip-cracker gone."

"It's been dead all afternoon. I was just trying to figure out something to do with my hair." Robin felt compelled to explain being caught looking in the mirror. She hadn't seen too much of Dr. Cook's wife since she'd been working for him, but she liked the bouncy, attractive young woman. Jan was so sure of herself that she could afford to be nice to everyone, and Robin desperately envied her for it.

Cocking her head to one side, Jan studied Robin with a bright-eyed, friendly stare. "You know what you need?" she said finally. "Different glasses. Those frames really don't do anything for you. No offense."

Robin pulled the glasses off again and frowned at them. Darned old things anyway. No matter what anyone told her, she was convinced that there was no such thing as a really pretty girl in glasses. If only she didn't have to wear them, it would make all the difference in the world. The frames, supposed to be clear plastic, were really pinkish-yellow, and getting yellower every year. She had chosen them three years ago, thinking they would be less conspicuous than dark ones.

Jan spoke again. "No kidding, Robin. Next time you get frames, why don't you try on some . . . oh, let's see . . . some of those little slanty ones with pretty side pieces, not ornate, but with some shape. Brown ones would bring out your eyes. You really have pretty eyes."

"Thanks." Robin put the hateful things back on and slouched down in Dr. Cook's chair. "Lot of good they do me." She sighed and fiddled with the arms of the chair.

"My, aren't we in the depths of gloom today! Boyfriend giving you a bad time?" Jan teased, not unsympathetically.

Robin stared at the black pen holder on the desk. "Hah. I've never had a boyfriend long enough for one to give me a bad time. In fact I've never even had a date." Oddly, it was a relief to tell somebody that.

"What are you, fifteen?"

Robin nodded and braced herself for a cheerful, "You have plenty of time for that."

"Heck, I know just how you feel," Jan said. "I never had a single date all the time I was in high school. People kept telling me I had plenty of time and all that, and as it turned out, they were right;

88

but it was miserable at the time. I always felt like my folks were watching me, wondering why nobody ever asked little Jan out. My older sister was quite popular."

Robin stared at the pretty woman perched on the desk, not quite believing her.

Jan chuckled, and a faraway look crossed her face. "No lie. I was the biggest social flop in school, till I got away on my own at college and sort of found myself. If that makes sense. I had to figure out just who Jan Vickers was, what kind of a person I wanted to be, and then to start *being* it, regardless of what my sister or my friends were."

She wriggled back on the desk. "I didn't mean to sound so profound. It was just part of growing up, and it took me longer than some of the other kids. But look what I ended up with—Tom, and the kids. . . ." Her eyes unfocused dreamily. "Lots of the popular kids in my class—you know, the upper crust —are divorced, a couple of them for the second time, and lots of them haven't done very much with their lives since high school. I'm just glad I'm me."

But that's you, Robin thought. Not me. And if I were Paul Carlisle, I wouldn't notice me either.

That night, while drying the supper dishes as her mother passed them to her, Robin said, "Mom, what would you think about my getting new frames for my glasses? I've had these for years, and the sides are getting awful wobbly. And I think they sit crooked." She took them off and wiggled the side pieces convincingly.

Mrs. Morgan rubbed at her nose with the back of her sudsy hand. Something about washing dishes never failed to make her nose itch. "You're earning your own money now, dear. You're certainly entitled to spend it any way you want. It seems a little foolish to get new frames unless you have to, but you do what you want. I think I'll let the skillet soak overnight. . . ."

NINE

Every morning for a week Cedar Grove shoppers and meanderers traveling the south block of the square passed the Morgan girl leaning against the shoe store window ledge, a large golden retriever at her feet. Gradually word got around that Robin was trying to cure her dog of being shy, and a few people began detouring past the pair bringing tidbits—meat scraps or dog biscuits borrowed from their own pets—to offer Kate.

By the end of the week, Kate spent her time sitting in front of Robin's legs instead of behind them, her bulk often resting squarely on the toes of Robin's loafers. She held still for head pats from strangers, toddlers as well as the old men who spent their days on the benches across the street by the bandstand. And the tidbit bringers were eventually rewarded with a wagging tail and a golden head stretched out toward them. Robin was quietly thrilled at Kate's progress, and she herself no longer shrank back inside when people looked at her, standing there.

Every day now Robin chose carefully from her closet before dressing. She still wore shorts and blouses; anything else on a fifteen year old in Cedar Grove in July would have been out of place. But now the shorts and blouses had to be clean and freshly ironed, and the blouse tails were tucked in. And every day she watched for a pink and white Chevy or a dark-haired pedestrian. But she didn't see Paul Carlisle again.

On Monday she used her free afternoon to study eyeglass frames and prices in Dr. Oberman's office on the west side of the square. There was a pair that caught her eye as soon as the office girl opened the display case. They fit Jan's description perfectly, with narrow up-slanted lenses and side pieces that were gracefully shaped and carved. The plastic was marbled, from a light tan that matched the highlights in her hair to the dark brown of her eyes. She tried them on, and they rode, light and glassless, like a feather on her nose.

"Those'll run you right around thirty-five dollars,"

Dr. Oberman said when he finally got around to waiting on her. "Your old lenses won't fit, and we'll have to have new lenses made. If you want, I can get them ordered today; be done by the first of next week."

Robin did some hasty mental subtracting. She had over a hundred dollars saved up already, intended for new school clothes in the fall. But glasses could come under the heading of clothes, she decided, looking with distaste at the old pinkish ones.

"Would you go ahead and order them please, and I'll pick them up next Monday."

The office girl made a note of the style number on the frames, and Robin left feeling good, as though she'd taken a definite step toward . . . something.

A few mornings later Paul Carlisle nosed his car into a parking place on the south side of the square, a little way down from where Robin and Kate stood. Turning off the ignition, he let the car coast till it bumped lightly against the curb. He swung the keys nervously, tapping them against the gear shift. He'd just casually walk past, on his way to the drugstore. It was perfectly logical that he might have an errand in the drugstore. He could stop to see the dog, and get to talking with Robin. . . .

In spite of all the moving around his family did, Paul never got used to being the new boy. And in a small town like this, it was murder. All the kids had

known each other all their lives. They'd started kin-
dergarten together, and learned to dance in the same
class in junior high, and all their folks knew each
other. Or else they were cousins.

By now, in high school, their social pattern was
set up, and even the kids who were at the bottom of
the stack *knew* who they were and where they fitted
in. Paul knew that once school started and he got
acquainted, it wouldn't be hard to sort them out, to
find his level somewhere around the middle and steer
clear of the extremes. But meanwhile it promised to
be a pretty lonesome summer.

Unless this Robin . . . He wished he knew how
old she was. She could be older than him, out of
reach. Or so much younger as to be outside the accepted limits of social customs. But she seemed nice,
and to go to all this trouble over a dog, she really
must love animals. She was certainly worth checking
out, anyway.

Paul had driven around the square at least twice
each day all week. In the afternoons she hadn't been
there, and on the occasions when she had been standing in front of the shoe store, Paul had lost his nerve
at the last minute and turned down Maple away from
the square. But by now his loneliness outweighed his
dread of meeting a new girl, and he stepped out of
the car, slamming the door firmly behind him and
walking away briskly.

Robin had been watching him from the corner of

her eye all the time he sat in the car gathering his nerve. Now, as he approached, she straightened her shoulders, pulled in her stomach a little, and prepared to speak first if necessary, rather than let the chance slip by.

But he spoke. "Hi," he said, stopping in front of Robin as though he had just noticed her. "Still at it, I see. How's she doing?" He kneeled, and Kate leaned toward him, sniffing his hand for dog biscuits. The number of people who brought her things was growing daily, and now she automatically and fearlessly searched every outstretched hand.

"She's coming along fine." There was pride in Robin's voice.

"Say, she sure is." Paul looked up at Robin, genuine pleasure in his voice.

While Robin told him about the people who brought Kate things to eat, he petted the dog, scratching under her ear. Then he stood and moved around till he was half sitting on the ledge beside Robin.

"How do you like Cedar Grove so far?" Robin asked, for lack of anything more clever to say.

"Fine. It's a nice town. Of course, it takes awhile to get acquainted."

"Where did you live before?" She twisted around to face him, and Kate curled up on the sidewalk between their feet.

"Omaha. My dad works for the telephone company. He was transferred here."

"Oh." She tried frantically to think of something to say so he wouldn't leave.

"What does your father do?" Paul asked, scratching nervously at his knee.

"He's retired. He used to work for the railroad."

"Oh." He cleared his throat and looked at the cars going by. "What year will you be in?"

"Sophomore next year."

"Oh." He brightened. "I'll be a junior." He asked about the school, and Robin answered as best she could. It was hard to describe Cedar when it was the only high school she'd ever gone to. School was school.

"It'll seem awfully small after Omaha," she finished lamely.

The conversation threatened to die then, but Robin couldn't stand the thought of him leaving now that they were just getting acquainted. So she said the first thing that came to her mind. "You must really like dogs."

"I sure do. All kinds of animals. I'm going to Iowa State when I graduate, and study veterinary medicine." He was openly enthusiastic now.

"You are? Really?" Robin was delighted. "I work for a veterinarian afternoons. Dr. Cook, down on Third and Maple."

"No kidding? You really *work* for one?" He regarded her with pleased envy. "Tell me all about it. What do you do?"

96

There were no conversational lags now. She talked, and he looked at her with growing respect.

"Do you think Dr. Cook would care if I stopped by some time when he isn't too busy?" he asked eagerly.

"No, he'd enjoy showing you around. Middle of the afternoon is usually pretty quiet, any day but Saturday." She beamed. Now they were getting somewhere.

"Say, I was just going down to the drugstore for a Coke. Want to come?" He stumbled a little over the rehearsed sentence, endearing himself to Robin.

"Yes, I'd love to, but . . ." They both looked down at Kate, lying between their feet.

"We could try taking her with us and tying her to the stool. The worst they can do is throw us out." His look was a challenge to Robin, and she rose bravely to meet it. So what if people stared at them, taking a dog into the drugstore! She'd be with Paul.

"Let's go."

Kate walked happily between them as far as the corner, but she balked at the door of the drugstore, with its strange sounds and smells.

"It's all right, Katy."

"Come on, girl; we're with you."

With both Robin and Paul reassuring her, Kate relented and followed them inside. Casually, Paul took the leash from Robin, tied it around the base of one of the stools at the counter, and sat down beside

97

Robin. The boy who took their orders, one of the kids in Robin's class, peered over the counter to look at Kate, but he made no objection to her being there. Robin leaned over her Coke to catch the straw in her mouth, rubbing Kate's ribs gently with the toe of her shoe and watching Paul out of the corner of her eye. He began to tell her about how he planned to work his way through college, and she drank in every word, proud that he would tell her about it.

After that, Robin quit taking Kate downtown mornings. Having made contact with Paul and letting him know where she worked so he could find her if he wanted to, she couldn't see much point in spending all that time downtown. Besides, Kate's attitude toward strangers had improved noticeably. She was still reserved, but anyone who would meet her halfway and pet her was rewarded with a friendly tail wag. She was openly affectionate only with Robin, but by now she trusted the girl completely.

Every afternoon that week Robin dressed with special care, in case Paul should drop in at the clinic. But he didn't come.

Saturday morning's mail brought a letter to Carter Crissman from Dale Cheevers. Mr. Crissman, in khaki pants and a brown plaid shirt, tipped back in his chair in the kennel office and ripped open the envelope.

Dear Mr. Crissman:

In answer to your letter of June 29, the golden retriever, Klondike Kate of Copper Lane, which I purchased from you a year ago last January, has been missing from my kennel for the past five months. You will recall in an earlier letter I advised you that the dog was timid to the point of being totally unmanageable. She therefore was worthless to me for either showing or breeding purposes, and when she attacked my kennel man for no reason, I ordered her destroyed. I am not a rich man, Mr. Crissman, and I cannot feed and house a worthless animal.

However, my kennel man advises me now that, as he was driving the dog to a place away from the kennel building where he could safely use the shotgun, she got away from him out the car window and ran off. It seems possible to me that this could be the same dog you wrote about.

I will be on a dog show circuit next week and will make it a point to stop and take a look at the dog. If she is finally coming out of her shyness as your letter suggests, it would be worth my while to have her back. I will of course reward the child who found her. Please send me the girl's name and address immediately, as I will be leaving here in a few days for the circuit.

Best regards,
D. Cheevers

Carter Crissman laid down the letter and stared out the window. What had he started? Why hadn't he just minded his own business and not written to the man in the first place. From the tone of the letter, it seemed obvious that the tightwad wasn't going to give Robin any breaks.

He passed a hand over his tan, freckled scalp and pondered the problem. One thing was certain. That dog belonged to Robin, not to Dale Cheevers, no matter what the AKC registration said. The only thing to do now was not to send Robin's address to Cheevers. That way the old so and so would have to come to him first. Then, if he couldn't talk Cheevers into dropping the whole thing, at least he could ride over to Robin's house with him to look at the dog and try to buy her back himself, rather than let Cheevers get his hands on her again.

Meanwhile, he'd have to warn Robin. Dreading this call more than any he'd made in years, Carter Crissman reached for the phone.

TEN

Robin sat on the small wooden stool in the corner of the clinic darkroom. She had just set the timer for six minutes and immersed an eight by ten sheet of film on a metal frame in the vat of developer fluid. A tiny red bulb over the vats gave off just enough light to emphasize the darkness of the closet-sized room. Today the blackness around her suited Robin's mood perfectly.

Ever since Saturday, when Mr. Crissman had told her about the man who might own Kate, losing her dog was all Robin could think of. Even though it had been in the back of her mind all along that Kate's owner might show up, to lose her now, when she was getting to like and trust people, was too awful to think about. Mr. Crissman had said not to worry, that he wouldn't let this guy take Kate, but Robin knew very well that if the dog was his, Mr. Crissman couldn't do anything about it. Some time around the end of the week he'd be coming. . . .

And as if that wasn't bad enough, here it was, five days since Paul had bought her the Coke in the drugstore, and she hadn't seen him since. She had been so sure he would stop by the clinic.

The bell on the timer rang. She stood up, lifted the frame out of the developer, and held the picture up against the red light. It was clear enough, the white outline of the tiny bones of a poodle's paw against the black background. She doused it thoroughly in the rinse water, then lowered the frame in the vat of fixer, set the timer for three minutes, and settled back on the stool again, feet against the vats.

The new glasses were the only bright spot in her otherwise bad week. As soon as she had gotten home with them Monday and tried them on in the privacy of her room, she knew they were right. Somehow they even seemed to draw attention to her eyes, rather than hiding them the way the old ugly ones had. These gave her a feeling of saying to the world, "Yes, I wear glasses. The prettiest ones in town. Want to make something out of it?" It was a good feeling.

But it couldn't offset the worry about Kate, and Paul. She would like to have stayed in the darkroom all afternoon, thinking dreary thoughts, but the three-minute bell went off, rousing her from the stool to fish out the frame and check the film. Seeing that it was fine, she settled back to wait out the final rinse. When that was done, she removed the frame from the water, tapping it against the rinse vat until the worst of the dripping was over.

Stepping out of the blackness into the glare of light in the hall, Robin nearly ran into Paul Carlisle. "Hi," they said together, embarrassed.

"Dr. Cook told me to look around," Paul explained, a little ill at ease from not having seen her for five days. "He went up to the house for something."

"Oh. Well, I'm glad you came." She blushed up at him, then noticed the puddle the dripping X ray was making on the hall floor. "Come on; I'll show you around."

She led the way into the examining room, hung up the X ray and frame, then took him on a quick tour of the building. There were nine dogs in the back room—four patients and five boarders—plus three cats and a raccoon. They stopped before each cage while Robin explained each occupant.

Paul was enthralled by the patients—the poodle with the crushed paw, the boxer with his newly trimmed ears bandaged over his head, and even

103

the small mongrel puppy still woozy from worm pills.

Once, Paul looked away from the cages to stare at Robin. "Say, you got new glasses, didn't you? Those are real sharp. I like 'em."

Robin thanked him and went on explaining about the dogs, holding the compliment in the back of her mind to take out and savor when she was alone.

In a few minutes Dr. Cook was back, three sweating cold bottles of pop swinging from his hand. "Well, Nurse Nelly," he said, grinning at them, "have you given this budding young horse doctor the fifty-cent tour of our little hospital? Good. Then come on in the office where we can all be comfortable."

They spent the rest of the afternoon, with occasional interruptions for business, talking in the office. Or more precisely, the men talked while Robin looked from one to the other, proud of both of them and of her position as employee of one and prospective girlfriend of the other.

Paul stayed till closing time, then offered Robin a lift home.

"You come back any time at all," Dr. Cook called after him as he locked the front door. "Might even put you to work, if you're not careful."

He watched while Paul held the door of the pink Chevy for Robin. They drove out onto Maple and headed west, Robin sitting stiffly on her side of the seat. Dr. Cook smiled a crooked little smile and sighed. That brought back memories. . . . Jan had been shy like that when they were first dating at college. Boy, how times do change! Whistling under his breath, he crossed the backyard.

Jan met him at the kitchen door. She stood on tiptoe for her kiss, stepping on his toes with her bare feet. "Honey, was that a *boy* Robin just drove off with?"

"That was exactly what that was, Charlie. A genuine, fourteen-carat boy. Real nice kid. He wants to be a vet. Spent the whole afternoon in there listening to my words of wisdom. What's for supper?"

"Pork chops. I'm sure glad Robin's got a guy hanging around her." Jan's eyes stared dreamily out the window as she tore at a handful of lettuce. She seemed to be remembering something, too.

A new white station wagon with two men in the front seat and several matched dog crates in the rear turned out of the Crissman driveway and headed north, toward Cedar Grove. On the side of the car, in gaudy black and gold letters, was written "Golden Gate Kennel, Chicago, Illinois."

Carter Crissman squirmed on his seat by the window, one arm outside, aware that Cheevers resented his presence. He had insisted on riding in with Cheevers on the excuse that it would be easier than trying to give him directions to the Morgan house. Actually, he had never been there himself, but it couldn't be too hard to find 510 Maple. Mr. Crissman had brought his checkbook and was quietly determined that Kate was going to stay out of the Cheevers kennel one way or the other.

Dale Cheevers, red-faced and beefy, gnawed at his cigar as he drove and silently hoped it would turn out to be a different dog. He'd about had a bellyfull of that Kate dog while he had her, always cringing away from him, crawling around on the floor, whimpering, not eating. You had to be firm with a dog like that. Not let it get away with that cringing. Never be a show dog that way. Three hundred bucks down the drain.

"Turn here, left," Mr. Crissman said. Then, "That yellow house, second from the corner."

Robin answered the door on the first knock. She stood aside, nodding politely at the introduction and smiling a thin, dry-mouthed smile at Mr. Crissman. She led the men into the living room, introduced them to her parents, and motioned them to sit down.

"I'll get Kate. She's around here somewhere." She went to the head of the basement stairs and called down. Kate was down there enjoying the bone from the supper roast where the grease wouldn't hurt anything. At Robin's call, she left the bone reluctantly and lunged up the stairs, wagging, ready for whatever Robin had in mind.

Hidden from the living room by the stairway

door, Robin kneeled quickly, fighting back the threatening tears, and buried her face in Kate's golden ruff. She hadn't really prayed in years, but tonight she sent up a fervent plea. "Oh, God, please, *please* don't let them take her."

Then, reluctantly, she got up. "Come on, Kate. We've got company." Patting her leg for Kate to follow, she went back to the living room. Kate trotted happily at her side, bumping Robin's knee as they rounded the hall corner. Then, suddenly, Kate froze.

Robin stopped beside her and looked from the dog to the men on the couch. She knew from Kate's reaction and from the look on Dale Cheevers' face. Kate was his. A sick feeling rolled over her, and she wondered fleetingly if she was going to vomit.

"That's her all right," Cheevers said pleasantly. "Here, Kate. Good dog." Kate backed up a step, trembling violently against Robin's legs. "Kate. Come here," Cheevers commanded. When Kate drew back even farther, he muttered something Robin couldn't hear. Standing up, he took a step toward the dog, and Kate was gone, down the basement stairs.

With barely concealed disgust at the dog's cowardice and, oddly, a brief moment of pity for the girl, Cheevers made his decision. "Tell you what, my dear." He smiled at Robin. "If you want to keep the little dog, I might sell her to you. You're probably attached to her by now, and I hate to split up a kid and her dog."

Robin sank to a chair, a cold sweat of relief breaking out all over her. "How much?" she asked weakly.

Cheevers grasped his knee and rocked back on the couch, staring thoughtfully at the ceiling. He had written the dog off as a loss, income tax wise, months ago when he thought she'd been shot. Anything he got for her now would be gravy. "She's a valuable animal, you know. I paid several hundred dollars for her a year ago. I couldn't take less than . . . fifty."

"I've got that much," Robin sang, bouncing out of her chair and up to her room. Luckily, she had converted her savings account to a checking account just last week.

Carter Crissman breathed an inaudible sigh of relief and took his hand away from the vicinity of his vest pocket. He had been prepared to go a lot higher than fifty if necessary.

Robin clattered down the stairs, checkbook in hand, and sat down at the desk in the corner to make out the check with shaking hands. She gave it to Mr. Cheevers, and he in return filled out the small white registration certificate he had brought along at the last minute, just in case.

At last they were gone. Robin, the precious certificate still clutched in her hand, smiled moistly at her parents, who had sat without speaking during the transaction. Then she turned and ran down to the laundry room where Kate had gone back to work on her bone, and, sitting on the cement floor with her back to the washer, she wrapped her arms around Kate's neck and cried unashamedly. Kate twisted around to lick at the tears, a worried expression creasing her big yellow face.

"It's okay, Katy, girl. This is happy crying. Now you're really, really mine."

ELEVEN

Now that Kate was officially hers, Robin was burning to enter her in a dog show. Of course there was still the problem of her fear of cars, but Kate had made such great strides toward becoming a well-adjusted member of society that nothing seemed impossible.

The next Monday afternoon Robin again made the glaring, dusty, three-mile hike to the Crissman home. It was now late July, and there was no escaping the muggy blanket of heat over Cedar Grove. By the time they reached their goal, Robin was dripping with sweat, and Kate was panting heavily.

They found Carter Crissman on a brightly flowered chaise lounge in the backyard, reading and swirling a glass of iced tea absentmindedly. He looked up as Robin crossed the lawn, and laid down his book, smiling in open pleasure.

"Hello there, dog owner. Figured you'd be along one of these afternoons. You look hot. Didn't *walk* all the way, did you?"

Robin grinned and nodded wearily, sinking into the other lounge. Mr. Crissman jumped up, went into the house, and returned with a glass of iced tea for Robin and a pan of water for Kate. Smiling her thanks, Robin mopped the sweat streaks from her face with the sleeve of her blouse.

Mr. Crissman sat down again, looking at Kate, who had finished the pan of water and was stretched out in the cool grass by Robin's chair. The cottonwood tree that spread over them gave a dense shade, and out here in the country there was a cool breeze that never quite penetrated the buildings in town.

"I was just wondering, Mr. Crissman," Robin began, making cold wet rings on her leg with the bottom of the glass. "Now that I own Kate officially, I sure would like to show her. Did you mean it when you said she was good enough . . ." Her voice trailed off.

"Of course she's good enough. She's a Copper Lane dog, isn't she? And she's by Campaigner. I know what." He leaned forward. "Our local kennel club is having a sanctioned match next month. They have one every year, usually over at Daws. But they

111

couldn't get the armory for the date they wanted this year, so they're going to have an outdoor match in McNeal Park. August . . . let's see . . . nineteenth, I think. Be the ideal time to try Kate. An outdoor show won't be nearly so frightening to her as an indoor one, with all its noise and confusion. And it would be close to home for you."

"What is a . . ."

"Sanctioned match? Most kennel clubs put on one a year, plus one regular show. At a sanctioned match there are no championship points, only ribbons. And any puppy over three months can enter. It's mainly for fun, and it gives puppies and beginners some ring experience before they tackle a real show." He leaned back and lit a cigarette.

"Also, the judges aren't official AKC judges, just professional handlers. I think it would be just the ticket for Kate. Frank and I'll be taking a couple of pups, and we'll be glad to help in any way."

Robin's eyes lit up. It was perfect. A small informal dog show within walking distance of home! And Mr. Crissman to help her.

"If it wouldn't be too much trouble," she said politely, "would you mind telling me everything I'll need to know to get Kate ready?"

Carter Crissman threw back his brown shiny head and laughed . . . harder than he had in years . . . since Margaret died. Then he got to his feet. "Come on into the kennel. We'll get you fixed up."

112

He led the way through the office to a small work-room in a corner of the building. Gently, he lifted Kate, who stiffened only slightly, onto a low, narrow table. He removed her collar and reached over her to a shelf which held a variety of combs, brushes, and scissors. Taking a large steel comb, he began working on the golden waves, talking softly to the dog as he worked. Robin stood at Kate's head, rubbing under her ears and watching.

"Say, you've been doing a good job of keeping up her coat. No mats anywhere."

Robin grinned proudly.

Taking a pair of toothed thinning shears from the shelf, Mr. Crissman said, "First thing to do is get rid of these tufty places in front of her ears." He worked the scissors through the base of the tufts, and the long hair disappeared, leaving a sleek, smooth surface of skull.

"Then, under her ears, all this excess coat. Now we'll shape the ruff, not take much off, you understand, just smooth the contours. Now a little off the tip of her tail, to make it shorter and fuller. Some off the hocks, like so."

Robin studied everything he did.

"Now, round off the shaggy places around her paws, and I . . . think . . . that . . . does it." He stood back and admired his handiwork. "She's a darned good golden when she's trimmed."

Robin stood back, too, as far as she could without letting go of Kate's neck. For the small amount of hair Mr. Crissman had removed, the results were surprising. Without the shaggy spurts of hair around her ears, Kate's head was smooth, finely molded, beautiful. Her ears lay low and flat against her head, and even her eyes seemed larger and prettier.

"Of course this will have to be done again a day or so before the show. Bring her out that Saturday, and we'll trim her up for you. All you'll have to do is give her a bath Saturday night, keep her brushed and combed between now and then, and she'll be ready. Except for ring training."

Robin was undaunted. "What's that, and how do we do it?"

"Come outside, and I'll show you." He led the way, smiling at the fun he was having.

Back in the shade of the cottonwood, he reached into his pocket and pulled out a lead. It was white nylon, about half an inch wide, with a loop in one end that was adjusted by a metal sliding clip. He slipped the loop over Kate's head, tightening the clip so she couldn't back out of it, and handed the other end to Robin.

"Be right back." He sprinted into the kennel, leaving Robin to stare, fascinated, at the lead in her hand. It felt so . . . professional. Then he was back, leading another golden on a similar lead. The two dogs touched noses, wagging tentatively, then ignored each other.

"Good," Mr. Crissman said. "At least she's not afraid of other dogs. That's a good sign. In fact, it seems to me that Kate isn't nearly so spooky as she was the first time you were out here."

"I've been taking her downtown every day to get her used to people. She's a lot better now." Robin spoke with pride.

"Good plan." He glanced at the girl. This Robin was no dummy. Had a way with dogs. He felt unexplainably proud of her.

He cleared his throat. "All right now. Wad the end of your lead up in your left hand. Like this. No loose ends. Now, slide the loop up under her neck so you've got control of her head. Keep it high. That's important. Hold your arm out away from your body so you don't get tangled up with her, and gait her in a straight line."

Grasping his lead and holding his arm out stiffly, he turned and walked away from Robin at a brisk clip. Straight toward the driveway, a sharp spin, then straight back. His dog trotted smoothly at his side, head high, mouth open in a tongue-lolling grin.

"He's beautiful," Robin breathed.

"Now you try. Remember, walk in a straight line and keep her head up."

It wasn't as easy as it looked to go straight, watching her dog and holding her arm out and keeping Kate's head up all at once. But she did her best, and Mr. Crissman didn't criticize.

115

After a few trips, he demonstrated with his dog how to pose Kate for the judge's inspection: front legs dropping squarely from her shoulders; back legs a little farther apart and back just enough to give her body a graceful flow; head high, not too far forward; tail held out even with her back.

"After she's learned to hold a pose," Mr. Crissman said, "it'd be a good idea to have your boyfriends go over her like a judge would—look in her mouth and so forth. Get her used to strange men touching her so she won't pull away from the judge at the match."

She nodded, pleased at his assumption that she had boyfriends. First with the other dog, then with Kate, she practiced the posing till she was sure she understood how it should be done. Then, not wanting to overstay her welcome, she thanked Mr. Crissman profusely for his help and began to exchange the show lead for Kate's own collar and leash.

"You keep that lead," he said quickly. "It's an old one, and we've got a dozen around here. If you have any problems, feel free to call or stop out."

"I don't want to be a bother." Robin flushed happily.

"No bother. I enjoy your company." He watched them go down the driveway and then went back toward the kennel, walking lightly across the lawn.

About four the next afternoon Paul stopped in at the clinic. Robin was especially glad to see him so she could tell him about buying Kate, and about the match next month.

"Hey, that's great." He beamed at the news. "Now we'll really have to work on her, with the training and all. What can I do to help?"

As easily as that, they became a team. Paul began coming over to Robin's house every morning for an hour or so, and most evenings after supper. It seemed to Robin that he was as excited about showing Kate as she was, and before long the dog was equally at ease with both of them.

Their morning sessions consisted of taking turns leading Kate around a square in the backyard, from porch to lilacs to dog pen to driveway to porch. Then Robin would pose Kate while Paul ran his hands over her and looked at her teeth. Gradually they lengthened the time Kate had to hold still, until she was steady for as long as they wanted.

And Kate loved every minute of it, even the tedium of standing still. She was the center of attention from her two favorite people, and their generous praise was music to the dog's ears. She was smart and anxious to please, and scoldings were seldom necessary.

In the evenings they usually had a short workout with the lead, then finished the long summer twilight on the back porch steps, talking dreamily about life and the future. Sometimes they put Kate in her pen and drove over to the root beer stand. The first time

117

she and Paul parked next to Dwight Wolber and Judy Braithewaite at the stand was one of life's small triumphs for Robin.

Those weeks of getting Kate ready for the match, and seeing Paul every day, were the happiest Robin could ever remember. The only thing that was the least bit wrong was that Paul never really treated her like a girlfriend, even though he was over almost every night. He never asked her for regular dates. "Oh well," she would tell herself, "at least he doesn't have time to find another girl. Not till we get Kate trained anyhow."

Then, suddenly, it was the middle of August, and the sanctioned match was next Sunday.

TWELVE

Kate, for all her progress in human relations, would still have nothing to do with cars, so that Saturday morning Robin was up at daybreak to walk the dog out to Mr. Crissman's for her trimming.

Since she had to be at the clinic at noon, she decided to risk going on her bike and letting Kate run along in the ditch. They took a gravel road that was very lightly traveled, and cut over to the highway just north of the Crissman kennel. Kate made the trip in fine style, hardly swerving when an occasional car rattled by on the gravel, smothering them in dust.

When Robin and Kate got to the kennel, they

found Frank and Mr. Crissman hard at work in the grooming room. They were bathing the two five-month-old puppies that were to make their debuts at tomorrow's match.

Mr. Crissman turned over his dripping pup to Frank for drying, and met Robin at the grooming room door. "Come in, come in. Hello there, Klondike Kate. All ready for your big day?" He lifted the dog onto the table as he had before, and repeated the trimming process, this time taking off each of Kate's whiskers, one by one, and the long stiff eyebrow whiskers with a small curved scissors. He was briskly professional today, and Robin instinctively felt that this was no day to linger and waste the men's time, even if she hadn't been in a hurry herself.

As soon as Kate was trimmed, Robin thanked Mr. Crissman again and again for his help and started for home, a cleanly trimmed Kate trotting happily beside her.

"Don't forget, be there before twelve tomorrow," Mr. Crissman called after them. He closed the kennel door and went back to work on his wet puppy.

It was a long afternoon. The clinic was unusually quiet for Saturday, and Robin spent more time glancing at the clock behind the reception desk than she did in actual work.

After supper, with Paul's help, Kate was bathed in the family bathtub, despite good-natured grumblings from Robin's parents. Secretly, they were so relieved at the change that had come over their daughter this summer, she could probably have bathed her dog in the middle of the living room floor without much comment from them.

The bath itself didn't take as long as cleaning up the bathroom afterward. By eight o'clock Kate was shampooed and towel-dried, and stretched out in damp contentment on the living room rug. Robin and Paul sat on the couch, brushing at wet spots on their clothes and laughing at how funny Kate had looked sitting soaked in the tub, with suds on her nose.

"Oh, boy," Robin sighed. "I don't know how I'm ever going to make it till tomorrow afternoon. Even if it is only a fun match, I'm so darned excited about it, I don't think I'll sleep tonight at all."

"Tell you what, it's early yet. Why don't we take a run out to the drive-in. I don't know what show is on, but we can kill a few hours anyhow. Maybe the movie will be boring enough to put you to sleep."

A date. A genuine date with Paul, just as she'd been hoping for. "I'll just get cleaned up a little and be right back." She bounded off the couch and ran up the stairs with Kate following, leaving a trail of wet paw prints on the bare wooden stairs.

Robin dug through her closet in a frenzy of inde-cision. What to wear . . . what to wear? She wished there was time to take a bath and do something with her hair. She had always imagined her first

121

date would have more leisurely preparations than this.

She decided on the white cotton sundress with brown embroidery that she had bought with her first clinic money and had had few excuses to wear. All the outside work with Kate had given her a better than usual tan, which the white dress set off surprisingly well. At least Robin was surprised. Maybe it was the new glasses, or the dress, or the excitement of a date with Paul, but for the first time, looking into the mirror, she was almost satisfied with the girl who looked back.

She tied her bath-dampened hair back with a white ribbon, carefully applied her lipstick, and stuck her bare feet into her best white flats. Then, Kate again behind her, she went downstairs, slowly this time.

"Shall we go?"

Paul stood, staring at this new Robin. It was the first time he had seen her dressed up, and she seemed like a stranger. "I like that dress," was all he could think of to say.

"Thank you, kind sir." If Robin had felt self-conscious a minute ago about going out with Paul, even though they were good friends on a buddy level, seeing him ill at ease now gave her a feeling of confidence, as though she were in command of the situation. It was a new feeling for Robin, and a good one.

Paul held the front door for her, closing it quickly before Kate could follow them out. Mr. and Mrs. Morgan were in the front yard, studying the bug holes in the rose bush leaves.

"Paul and I are going out to the drive-in. Is it okay?" Robin suddenly realized she should have asked them before she changed her clothes.

Mrs. Morgan glanced at her husband to read his expression. She said, "I expect that'd be all right, but don't forget you've got a big day tomorrow. Drive carefully, won't you, Paul."

The two senior Morgans watched the car back out of the driveway. Then they turned, slipping arms about each other's waists, and walked slowly across the yard to the porch.

The movie was a western. Jimmy Stewart. It was a good show, Robin was dimly aware. Her heart was pounding, and her hands were folded in her lap to keep them from fidgiting at being here, in the dark of Paul's car.

She sat exactly one foot from the door, in what she figured was the right place, neither so far from Paul as to look standoffish, nor so near as to be bold. The full skirt of her dress spread from the car door clear over to Paul's knee.

He sat behind the wheel, one arm over it, the other hung limply over the gear shift. From time to time he cleared his throat or shifted in the seat, and every few minutes he glanced at Robin from the corner of his eye. Gee, she had a cute profile. He was glad he'd worn a fairly nice sport shirt tonight.

About halfway through the first feature he stretched elaborately and let his arm fall back along the seat. His legs were cramped, so he squirmed around to stretch them out as best he could. He felt he was handling the whole thing badly, especially for a guy who was almost a junior, but the truth was that this was his first actual date. What with moving from one school to another, always being the new guy, and being by nature slow at making friends, Robin was the first girl he had ever really been on talking terms with. Even at that, if he hadn't had the excuse of helping train Kate, no telling how long it might have taken to get to the dating stage.

Robin saw him stretch and felt his hand resting on the seat behind her head. She wanted to move over closer to him, but she didn't dare take that first big step. After a while she felt his fingers toying with a strand of her hair; then his hand was resting ever so lightly on her right shoulder. She recrossed her legs, moving an inch closer to him. He stretched his legs into a more comfortable position and moved an inch closer to her.

Then the movie ended. The cartoons came on, and the advertising for the refreshment stand. Paul thought he should offer to go get popcorn or something, but he didn't want to move and lose the ground he had gained. So they sat, staring at the screen through the intermission and previews. Well into the second feature, he gathered his courage and reached over, gently lifting off Robin's glasses. She turned to him, startled, and he kissed her.

Registration for the Cedar Valley Kennel Club's Fifth Annual All Breeds Sanctioned Match was held from eleven to twelve o'clock, on a picnic table in McNeal Park. Admission was free, registration a dollar per dog.

Robin stood in line, her dollar in hand, while Kate sat on her foot taking in the scene. Her anticipation was beginning to curdle at the sight of so many people with so many dogs, all of whom obviously knew exactly what they were doing.

Some men were pounding stakes into the ground and tying ropes from stake to stake to form four squares, each about twenty feet across. Those were the rings, Robin supposed. Somehow she had envisioned one large round ring, like the one she had seen once at a horse show. How did people know which ring to go to?

People were everywhere under the trees, clustered around dog crates of various sizes and descriptions. On top of many of the crates dogs were standing while their owners worked at them with combs and scissors and chalk blocks. Robin had spotted several other golden retrievers, but no Mr. Crissman or Frank yet.

Then she was facing the two women seated at the picnic table. "Name?" one of them asked. "Address? Dog's name and AKC number?"

Robin fished the white slip from her purse. "Klondike Kate of Copper Lane, S-256876."

The woman wrote it down. "What class?"

Robin looked at her blankly.

"How old is the dog?" the woman asked, her voice edged with impatience.

"Two years."

"You want her in Open, then?"

Robin nodded, wondering what Open was.

Leaving the table, she saw Mr. Crissman and Frank coming toward her, each leading an excited young golden.

"Good. You made it," Mr. Crissman called. "What class you sign up for?"

"Um—Open."

"Fine, fine. Guess I forgot to explain the different classes to you. Chances are there'll just be Puppy and Open classes. In a bigger show, there'd be more. Well, Frank, we'd best get in line. Wait here, Robin, and you can eat lunch with us. Brought plenty."

Robin led Kate to a nearby picnic bench and sat down, careful not to get anything on her skirt. She had forgotten about lunch. Paul's parents had insisted that he eat Sunday dinner at home, but he had promised to be here just as soon as he could get away.

When Mr. Crissman and Frank had passed through the registration line with their pups, Robin followed them back to where their car was parked, a little distance from the center of activity. She tied Kate to a sapling a few yards from the car, and the men herded their pups into two attractive plywood crates that stood beside the station wagon.

"Judging won't begin for an hour or so," Mr. Crissman said, fishing a picnic hamper from the front seat of the car. "They'll judge each breed separately and get the Best of Breed dogs. Then they'll go for best of each of the six groups, then Best in Match. Process of elimination."

He handed Robin a thick roast beef sandwich and took out one for himself and one for Frank, who had settled down comfortably on one of the crates. Mr. Crissman sat behind the steering wheel of the car, half in and half out of the open door. Robin sat hunched on the other crate, where she could keep an eye on Kate while she forced down the dry sandwich.

Before, she hadn't really been nervous about showing Kate, but now that the time was at hand, she was developing stage fright. The whole thing was so complicated—the different classes, and all the instructions Mr. Crissman had given her about what to do in the ring. It was only a fun show, she reminded herself firmly. Nothing to be scared about.

The sandwich just wouldn't go down. She ate

as much as she could, then tossed the rest to Kate when no one was looking. Why didn't Paul hurry up and get here? And why didn't they start the judging and get it over with? She could have been spending a nice relaxed Sunday afternoon at home reading, instead of being out here about to make a fool of herself doing something she knew nothing about and at which everybody else was an expert.

At long last a young man in a loud plaid sport coat mounted one of the picnic tables and called for attention through a megaphone.

"The Cedar Valley Kennel Club would like to thank you all for turning out today. We have 243 entries, making this our largest sanctioned match ever.

"Now, before I announce the order of judging, I want to remind you all of the Des Moines show, which will be held October fifth in the Varied Industries Building of the Iowa State Fairgrounds. Most of the puppies here today will be old enough for a licensed show by then, so let's have a big turnout from Cedar Valley.

"Today's judging will proceed as follows: Sporting Group first, breeds in alphabetical order; Hound Group second . . . "

Mr. Crissman folded himself out of the car and closed the door. "Sporting Group first. That's us. We'll be right after the German shorthair pointers." He and Frank went to work immediately, lifting their dogs up on the crates and brushing them vigorously.

Robin stood aside, helpless. She was sure she should be doing something to Kate.

All through lunch she had been hoping her class would be one of the first, to get it over with, but now that it was, she wished desperately that she could have had time to watch some of the others before her turn in the ring. And why didn't Paul hurry? He could at least be some moral support.

"Want a comb?" Frank held out a big steel comb. "Got a few stomach butterflies?"

Robin nodded and took the comb. She urged Kate to her feet and bent awkwardly over her to comb out the feathering on her forelegs.

"Ain't a person here that's completely calm," Frank went on kindly. "Even us old pros. Ain't that right, boss?" Mr. Crissman nodded absently as he worked. "Remember, this is only for fun, and for ring experience for you and the dog. Even if you do lousy, ain't nobody going to notice much, excepting you. But I'll tell you, that Kate dog's got both of these pups beat. She'll do okay."

Robin didn't really believe him, but she felt a little better. She handed back the comb, and Frank passed her a brush. As she brushed Kate's back and sides, Robin could see the first classes filing into the rings. In the nearest of the four rings were two liver and white English pointers, so she assumed that was her ring. There were dogs in the other rings, too, but she didn't look farther than the pointers.

129

She gave the brush back to Frank and straightened up, leaning against the crate. She was trembling all over, and she knew she would never be able to walk into that ring.

THIRTEEN

Then Paul was there, smiling and happy and anxious for Kate's turn in the ring. "You look a little pale, Rob," he said after she introduced him to Mr. Crissman and Frank. "You feel okay?"

"First-show nerves," Frank interrupted. "She wouldn't be human if she didn't have 'em."

Robin gave him a sick smile. "Mr. Crissman, maybe it would be better, for Kate's first show, if somebody who knew how would show her. Do you think you could . . ." Her voice trailed off, and she dropped her eyes.

Mr. Crissman slipped a lead over his dog's head and let the pup jump to the ground. For the first time all day he turned his full attention to the girl. "Now, Robin, that's no way to talk. I've seen you work with Kate, and, believe me, you handle the dog as well as anyone could. Besides, I doubt that Kate would let anyone else show her, or if she did, she'd be looking around for you when she should be paying attention to her business."

He stared at Robin until she was forced to look up at him. "Now let's see that smile of yours. There now, that's better. They're through with the English pointers, and I think there's only one shorthair ahead of the goldens. We'd better be getting up to ringside. Come along, young man," he said to Paul. "We'll need you for a cheering section."

The four moved across the grass to stand near the entrance to their ring. Robin fussed over Kate, trying to keep her from sitting down and getting uncombed, but the dog was taking the whole thing pretty much in her stride. Beneath her own tension, Robin was happily surprised that Kate was so calm.

The lone German shorthair pointer was in the ring, being posed before the judge, a small, thin man who walked in a habitual stoop.

Mr. Crissman moved closer to Robin. "All the male goldens will be judged first, then the females. You just watch Frank and me, and do what we do. Quite a few goldens here." He looked at the dozen or so people around them, each with a golden retriever in tow.

132

The German shorthair was leaving the ring with his handler and their automatic first place ribbon, and Mr. Crissman and Frank, the only entries in their class, were circling briskly inside the roped-off square. The judge watched the two dogs for several laps, then held up his hand. The men halted and posed their pups as best they could, but the youngsters were wound up with excitement and refused to hold still. One of them jumped up against the judge as he leaned over to make his examination, and the judge was kissed wetly on the nose.

But the judge was prepared for the antics of puppies of this age. He batted gently at the puppy's nose, just hard enough to let the pup know this was serious business, and went on with his examining. In a few minutes he handed the first place ribbon to Mr. Crissman.

Next came Open Dogs. One class nearer to Kate's. There were five in this class, and they were more mature and better behaved. But Robin was surprised to see that two of them hadn't been trimmed, and one of the others was so big and dark that he could almost have passed for an Irish setter. It was heartening to find out they weren't all perfect.

When the winner was chosen, the other four were dismissed from the ring, and Mr. Crissman went back in with his puppy to try for Winners Dog. All the studying that Robin had done in the pamphlet Mr. Crissman had given her was coming back to her now.

It had been confusing when she read it, but now that she saw it in action, the progression of classes began to make some sense.

The winner of the Open class was awarded Winners Dog, and Mr. Crissman came out and handed his pup's lead to Frank. Their dogs were through now and could go back to their crates.

Robin tried to think of something to say to console Mr. Crissman for not having won, but one look at his face told her it wasn't necessary. It was all in a day's work for him. He looked down and caught Robin's expression.

"I didn't expect my five-month-old to win over a good mature dog like that." He smiled at her. "Both the pups showed well and got a taste of the ring. That's all we came for."

Now the Puppy class for females was in the ring. Two pups, one still round and furry and the other full grown but sparsely coated, were in the ring.

"No competition there," Mr. Crissman whispered. "The big one will get it, but she won't stand up against Kate."

The big one did get the blue ribbon. Both puppies left the ring, and it was time.

"Go get 'em, Rob," Paul said, patting her quickly on the shoulder.

"Just take it easy. Kate's the best dog in the class." Mr. Crissman gave her arm a little squeeze for luck, and to get her started into the ring.

There were three dogs ahead of her. As soon as Robin and Kate entered, the judge waved his arm, and the four teams moved out at a fast walk around the ring. The lead was a moist wad in Robin's hand, but she managed to keep her arm up and out, and to follow the dog in front of her. At least I didn't have to go first, was all she could think of as they circled.

Kate was trotting close to Robin's legs, and her tail was down, but other than that, from what Robin could see between watching the judge and the man in front of her, Kate was doing fine.

At the judge's signal the four handlers—two men, one middle-aged woman, and Robin—halted. Following the others' example, Robin kneeled beside Kate, who promptly sat down. Red-faced, Robin slid her hand under Kate's stomach and gave her a quick little jab with her thumb. Kate stood, surprised.

Robin worked the lead up high under Kate's ears and, with her left hand, smoothed the ruffled hair over the crest of her neck. Then, as she and Paul had done so many mornings, she set Kate's feet in their correct positions. She grasped Kate's tail and held it out, her right arm aching from the weight of Kate's head against the lead. The dog stood calmly enough, moving only her eyes as she watched the dog ahead of her.

The judge stood across the ring from them, his eyes darting from one dog to the next, his hands clasped behind his back, lips moving in and out as he studied.

Assured that Kate was posed correctly, Robin stole a quick look at the other dogs. One wasn't trimmed. In fact she didn't even look combed. Robin passed over her, feeling superior. The other two were bigger than Kate. One was way too big, rawboned and harsh-looking.

The judge came down the line now, going over each dog carefully with his hands. Just before he got to Kate, she moved one hind leg forward. She was tired of standing still. Robin replaced it, suddenly sensing that Kate was about to sit down. The judge was still looking at the third dog. Robin let go of the hind leg and touched Kate's stomach lightly with her thumb. Remembering the poke she had gotten when she sat down before, Kate changed her mind. When the judge got to them, Kate was posed perfectly.

It was a tense moment for Robin as the man reached for Kate's head. She felt the dog stiffen, but the four golden feet held steady; Kate allowed him to part her lips to see that her teeth met in a perfect scissors bite. She held her stance while strange hands passed over her head and shoulders and down one front leg. The judge tested the spring of her ribs and the firmness of her hocks. Then, with a friendly pat on her rump, he straightened and moved to the center of the ring.

"Take them around again please," he called.

Knees popped as the four handlers rose, and the retrievers gratefully broke their stances to surge around the ring again. Kate was accustomed to the place and the smells and the noises by now, and this time she gaited with her tail high and swinging with every step.

After a few laps they were halted again, and the judge took four ribbons from a card table in one corner of the ring. All the handlers watched tensely as he returned to them. Ribbons in hand, he walked down the line, stopped before Robin, and held out the bit of blue satin. He moved on up the line, but Robin didn't see him. She stared at her hand and the blue ribbon.

She had won. She and Kate had actually won the class! She couldn't believe it. When she looked up, the other three were gone and the winner of the Puppy class for females was back. They repeated the circling and posing, and the purple Winners ribbon was in Robin's hand with the blue. She felt dizzy. The other dog left the ring, and Robin started to follow.

"Just a minute, miss." The judge's voice stopped her. "Stay in the ring please, for Best of Breed."

Robin barely had time to be embarrassed at her mistake before the dog that had beaten Mr. Crissman's puppy was in the ring. Heady with success, Robin was rather expecting to win again, and she

137

was sharply disappointed for an instant when the Best of Breed ribbon went to the other handler. But she managed to smile at the man as they left the ring.

"You did great, Rob!" Paul's voice crackled with excitement as he fell in step beside her. Mr. Crissman and Frank walked on the other side of her as they all headed automatically for the Crissman car.

"That was a good handling job, young lady." Mr. Crissman beamed down at her as they walked. "Wouldn't have been surprised to see you go all the way, but then the other dog was a beauty, too. Had this been a regular show, Kate would have three points toward her championship."

Robin stopped, then walked on slowly. Three points, just like that. She knew from the pamphlet that it took fifteen, with at least two three-point wins, to make a champion. For the first time it didn't seem impossible that Kate could do it. She and Kate, together.

The summer had just gotten a good start, and now, suddenly, it was late August. The stores downtown were already displaying wool skirt and sweater sets and dark fall cottons.

Robin, fired with enthusiasm by Kate's success at the sanctioned match, was aiming all her daydreams at the big Des Moines show in October. Thinking about school and the necessity for new fall clothes was just a lot of bother. Besides, she was inwardly dreading the start of school for another reason.

All summer she had had Paul to herself, mainly because he didn't know anybody else. Now that they didn't need to work on Kate every day, he still came over most evenings, which should have reassured her, but didn't. As soon as school started and all those other girls began making a fuss over him, he'd forget all about Robin Morgan.

Jan Cook and Robin were in the clinic office, enjoying their afternoon Coke break, a tradition that had grown during the summer. Often Paul managed to drop in about the same time, with ice cream bars or Popsicles from the cart that patrolled Maple Street all summer.

He and Dr. Cook had become good friends just as Robin and Jan had. Dr. Cook was still new enough at being a veterinarian to enjoy Paul's hero worship and intelligent questions, and Jan liked to think she was helping Robin develop a new personality.

But today Paul was mowing the lawn at home, and Dr. Cook was in the house napping, but on emergency call. He had been awake most of the night with Brucie's stomachache. Jan had, too, but the lack of sleep didn't bother her.

She sat on her husband's desk and studied Robin. The glasses had helped, and during the summer Robin had lost a few pounds in the right places. She stood up straighter now, too, and had a little more confident manner. But there were still a few things. . . .

"Robin, you know what you need before school starts?"

"Yeah." Robin grinned wryly. "A new fall coat, three wool skirts, at least two new blouses, shoes . . ."

"No, seriously. You need a new hairdo. No offense."

It didn't occur to Robin to be offended. She was hungry for suggestions. "How do you think I should fix it?"

Jan cocked her head and pulled her mouth around to one side of her face. "Ummm. I think if I were you, I'd . . . cut it off real short on the sides, leave some height on top, loose waves . . ."

Robin frowned. "Gee, I don't know. I was going to let it grow long. Most of the sharp kids have their hair long now."

"So?"

Robin shrugged helplessly.

"Who are you, Robin Morgan or the rest of the kids? Take it from old Mother Cook. Your hair is too thin and fine to look good long. It would just droop. It's beautiful hair; in fact I wish mine was that fine and soft. But I think it would be better for you short. Your face is kind of round, and if you had your hair higher on top and flat on the sides, it would balance things out."

Robin shut her eyes and tried to picture it. Maybe Jan was right.

140

"If you'd trust me to cut it, why don't you come over tonight after supper, and we'll get out the old poodle scissors?"

Robin thought a minute. "You've got yourself a customer, ma'am."

That night, seated in the middle of the Cooks' huge old-fashioned kitchen, Robin surrendered her head to Jan's barber scissors. Dr. Cook put the boys to bed, then sat at the table with a cup of coffee and made encouraging remarks from time to time.

Jan worked quickly, skillfully, surprising even herself. "I may hang out a shingle and go into business for myself. I knew I was a whiz at little boys' crew cuts, but I didn't know I was this talented."

When her victim was shorn and shampooed, Jan set Robin's hair carefully, sometimes pulling out a curl to redo it in a different direction. "There now," she said finally. "Go home and sleep on it and come over the first thing in the morning so I can see what I did."

Robin was up early the next morning. Standing in front of her dresser, she pulled out the pins and hoped for the best. With school starting next Monday, if her hair turned out awful, there wouldn't be much time to do anything about it. She brushed it out thoroughly, then combed it into place.

Breathlessly, she surveyed her hairdo. It was okay. In fact, it was beautiful. Grabbing a hand mirror, Robin twisted around till she had studied her new head from every angle. The crown waved back gently from her forehead, falling in soft golden-brown curves on the sides. The lower sides curled sleekly back behind her ears, making her face look narrower. Even the glasses seemed less conspicuous now, surrounded by this soft gold-glinted cloud.

Holding her head high, she went down to the kitchen to show her mother. She could hardly wait to surprise Paul. For the first time she began to think she had a fighting chance to hang onto him even after he was exposed to the rest of Cedar Grove's female population.

FOURTEEN

Tuesday morning, the day after Labor Day. The end of summer and the beginning of being a sophomore.

Paul stopped to pick Robin up promptly at eight-fifteen, looking especially neat in a muted blue plaid shirt and dark blue slacks. This time he wasn't dreading his first day in the new school. At least, not nearly as much as he would if it weren't for Robin. Of course they'd probably be in different classes, but at least he wasn't going in cold this time.

Robin met him at the door before he had a chance to knock. "I'm all ready, so we may as well get started." There was a little nervous edge to her voice, but it was as much anticipation as anything. Not that there was anything to get worked up about, going back to Cedar Grove Consolidated High School. Except for a few new kids who may have moved to town during the summer, she knew everybody in the school. But between the clinic and Kate and Paul, she had hardly seen any of the others all summer, and everyone would have grown a little, changed a little.

She was certain she had changed, in more ways than the glasses and hairdo and suntan. Since last spring Robin Louise Morgan had been offered a job, had learned to do, and to do well, things that most of the other kids knew nothing about. Running blood tests, keeping books for a business, handling irate clients and weeping children who had lost a pet, learning not only to stay conscious during bloody operations but to watch with curiosity and even to assist. She had met an attractive boy and been able to make a friend of him, if not quite a boyfriend yet. And she had taught a frightened animal to trust her and other people.

It seemed like quite a bit for someone like her to have accomplished. But on the other hand, this new self-trust had yet to be tried against the kids at school. Some of them had spent the summer traveling with their parents, some working at more glamorous jobs than Robin's. They all would have matured during the summer, possibly much more than she had. She might even be farther behind this year than last in Cedar's social scheme.

At least she was riding to school with a boy. That was something. She directed Paul down the side street and into the student parking lot. He parked, jumped out, and ran around to Robin's side of the car to open the door for her. She slid awkwardly out.

"I guess I'll have to go to the principal's office first, and give them my transcript," Paul said as they crossed the gravel toward the old brick building.

"I'll show you where it is." They were ill at ease with each other, yet at the same time drawn together, apart from the others, Robin remembering previous years' slights and exclusions and Paul wary of new ones.

They climbed the broad concrete steps, Robin briefly greeting groups they passed, wondering if she should stop and introduce Paul. But it was easier not to, so they went on into the building and up to the principal's office on the second floor. The halls echoed with loud greetings and clashing locker doors, and the smell of fresh floor wax was everywhere.

Outside the office door they stopped. "Well, good luck," Robin said. "Maybe we'll have a class together."

"I sure hope so." He felt as though he were about to lose his only friend. "Want a ride home at noon?"

"Sure. If you want to take me . . ." She didn't want to be a pest to him, or have him feel he had to haul her around just because of this summer.

"Of course I want to. Meet you at the car."

145

Within a few days Paul Carlisle, the new junior boy, had been assimilated into the high school. The girls did a lot of talking among themselves about how cute he was, but before long they realized that Robin Morgan had a prior claim, and they accepted him as nice but unavailable.

It seemed to Robin that things were looking brighter this year. Judy Braithewaite and her crowd were a little friendlier, especially when word got around that she was going with Paul. And Dwight Wolber, last year's source of misery for Robin, was finding excuses to walk from room to room with her, and ask questions about assignments. She had the feeling he would ask her for a date if she gave him a little encouragement, but his blond good looks seemed shallow now, compared to Paul. In fact, it was hard to remember now why she'd had such a crush on Dwight last year. Perhaps just because he was one of the leaders.

On Saturday afternoon, Robin was back at work in the clinic. Dr. Cook had asked her to go on working Saturdays through the school year. "In fact," he had said, "I believe next summer we'll go whole hog and get you some white uniforms. You'll add a little class to the joint, Nurse Nelly." She was relieved that he was planning to keep her on through the winter, and next year. She'd hesitated to ask, but the longer she worked for him, the more she loved the job.

The first Saturday after school started Carter

Crissman dropped in at the clinic. He waited politely until Robin made change for a departing client.

"Good luck with the new puppy," Robin called after the woman, then turned to Mr. Crissman. "Hi. What can we do for you today?"

"Came to see you, not Tom." He handed her a small leaflet. "Thought you might need this. Premium list for the Des Moines show."

"A what?" She flipped through the leaflet.

"Premium list. Has the entry blanks in the back. Gives all the information—time, date, place, list of judges, lists of trophies and cash prizes. Even tells what hotels and motels near the show will accept dogs. Everything you need to know." He took it from her and turned to the entry blanks in the back. "You did say you wanted to enter Kate?"

Robin nodded emphatically.

"Fill this out, and send it with six dollars to this address here. That's the company that handles the details of the show. Entries have to be in before September twenty-fifth. Frank and I'll be glad to trim her again. Other than that, give her all the exercise you can. Sporting breeds should be hard-muscled."

Robin nodded again, excitement mounting. By now she had completely forgotten the agony of stage fright that she had gone through at the match.

"Another thing, you and your young man might come out a few Sundays. We'll get out the pups and

147

work them with Kate. Let them all get used to posing and gaiting with strange dogs."

"Oh, that'd be wonderful, if it wouldn't be too much bother."

"No bother. My pups need the practice worse than Kate does. How about tomorrow?"

"Fine. We'd love to."

Paul was enthusiastic when Robin asked if he wanted to go to the Crissman kennel to school dogs. "But how are we going to get Kate out there?" he asked. "For that matter, how are you going to get her to Des Moines for the show? That's less than a month away, and she isn't any better about cars than she was last spring."

Robin sighed. It was true. "Well, let's try again tomorrow to get her into your car. If she just won't, I'll ride my bike, and you can drive alongside."

Paul was at the Morgan house right after Sunday dinner, and the two of them coaxed and reasoned with Kate for half an hour, but she would come no closer than six feet of the car. They led her around it. Robin got in and sat with the doors open calling to her. They tried dog biscuits, gentleness, firmness, even light spanks. The elder Morgans watched from the side porch, shaking their heads in sympathy. But Kate was adamant. Cars meant nothing but fear and pain to her, and even Robin couldn't convince her otherwise.

Finally, grumbling in exasperation, Robin wheeled her bike out of the garage and gave Paul instructions about which road to take. They started off, Paul driving slowly ahead, Robin pedaling behind with one eye on the leg of her slacks that threatened to catch in the bicycle chain, and Kate trotting happily in the ditch. She enjoyed the leg-stretching three-mile run, with its rabbit tracks to sniff and birds on fence posts to bark at.

Frank gave Robin a sympathetic grin as she dismounted and leaned her bike against the kennel building. He had been raking the first fall of leaves at the side of the house when the cavalcade drove, pedaled, and trotted up the drive.

"I see Kate still ain't riding in no cars," he called.

Robin wiped at her dusty forehead. "She won this round, Frank, but don't worry. I'll get her used to cars before the show, or know the reason why."

Paul parked the car and came toward them just as Carter Crissman came out the back door of the house. "Well, well. All ready to go to work? Nice to see you again, young man. Forgotten your name." He and Paul shook hands.

"Paul Carlisle, sir."

"Oh, yes. Shall we get started?"

Frank brought out the two puppies they had shown at the match, and with Kate they went through the motions of a dog show class on the graveled area in front of the kennel. First Paul acted as judge;

149

then Frank and Mr. Crissman each took his turn while Paul led a puppy. They worked for half an hour or so, then took a break, sitting in the lawn chairs and letting the dogs rest in the grass.

"Kate is coming on very well," Mr. Crissman said to Robin. He had to lean to one side to see past Paul, who sat on the foot of his chaise lounge, playing with one of the pups. "You do a good job handling her, too. She still tenses when the judge comes at her, but a few more Sundays out here should help that. When you have her posed, watch that she doesn't relax and let her back sag. She did that once today, and it made her look swaybacked."

Robin nodded and made a mental note. Watch her back.

"As for conformation," he continued, "she's a hard dog to fault. She needs more hardening, though. Roadwork is the best thing for that, so you might let her run alongside your bicycle some every day. Aside from that, if you can keep her from appearing timid in the ring, she should be hard to beat. I'm glad I won't be showing against her."

Robin smiled at the compliment and made more mental notes. Roadwork, don't let her seem shy, watch her back. "Let's practice some more, shall we?"

The days fell into a pleasant pattern for Robin. Every afternoon she and Kate headed out of town for an hour of roadwork that built up Robin's muscles

150

as much as the dog's. Most evenings Paul brought his homework over to do with Robin, and once a week they had a regular dress-up date. Saturday afternoons were work times, and Sundays Robin and Paul spent at the Crissman kennel, schooling the three dogs.

Her schedule didn't leave much time for extra-curricular school activities, but she and Paul managed to go to the important football games and the dances afterward. When Robin remembered the sock hop last spring, and how miserable she had made herself over it, she had to smile. She'd been so much *younger* then.

Kate's entry was sent in for the Des Moines show, and a week before the big day Robin received her confirmation from the dog show company with two free admission tickets, a slip saying that Klondike Kate of Copper Lane was Golden Retriever Number Nine, and a copy of the judging schedule. She read through it quickly . . . golden retrievers, thirteen entered, to be judged at two-thirty. Mr. Wilson Abernathy, judge.

Just one more week. This time there was no fear of the unknown to spoil Robin's anticipation of the show. Mr. Crissman had assured her there would be little difference between the sanctioned match and a regular show, as far as ring procedure was concerned. He had invited Robin, Paul, and Kate to ride to Des Moines with Frank and himself Sunday morning, and had promised to lend Robin a crate for Kate to stay in once they got there.

Now all she had to worry about was how to get old stubborn Katy into the car Sunday morning.

FIFTEEN

Monday afternoon Robin walked home from school slowly, scuffling through the bright, brittle leaves on the sidewalk. Paul now had a job after school, at the dry cleaners, to build up his college fund, so she was back to walking home from school.

The problem today was whether or not to give Kate her roadwork. The dog was in as good a condition as she was going to get before Sunday, and it seemed like a waste of a beautiful fall afternoon. Still, there wasn't much to do around the house. I'll take her out to McNeal Park and back, she finally decided. The trees should be gorgeous by now, and that won't be too long a ride.

The trees in the park were indeed gorgeous, with all their mingling shades of gold and crimson and brown. In fact they were so pretty that it was nearly dusk when Robin and Kate started back toward town. It was a perfect afternoon, and with the show only six days away, and things going so well with Paul, Robin couldn't help singing as she pedaled down the deserted road.

She let her arms fall to her sides and leaned back, unconsciously picking up speed down a slight incline. Kate was ranging ahead, barking furiously at anything that moved, and looking back now and then to make sure Robin was coming.

As the bicycle neared a low concrete culvert over a narrow creek bed, the cuff of Robin's slacks flapped into the bike's chain, caught, and jammed the back wheel to a stop so suddenly that Robin and the bike flew into the air and down the side of the ditch, which dropped off sharply at the creek. Robin's head grazed the edge of the culvert, and she and the bicycle landed in a tangled heap, her legs and the back wheel in the water.

At the clatter behind her Kate whirled and loped back toward the culvert. Robin was lying face down in the long grass, the front wheel of the bicycle still spinning in the air.

Wagging happily, Kate slid down the embankment. This was a game the girl often played with her, lying on the floor, hiding her face, and making teasing noises until Kate's nose and tongue found a way to get in and lick, turning the teasing noises to smothered giggles.

Kate licked at Robin's face now, but the girl didn't move. Slowly, the dog's tail quit wagging, and she pawed at Robin's arm, whining. Still she didn't move. Perplexed, Kate sat down to stare at Robin, head tilted to one side, a frown wrinkling the big yellow face.

A car was coming. Kate stood up suddenly and climbed the bank. She trotted to the middle of the road, then paced back and forth nervously as the car approached. Her heart was pounding with fear, but she stood firmly in the road and barked as the car slowed down, swerving to miss her, and went on.

Another car came, and another. Both slowed, detoured around the big yellow dog in the road, and passed her. "Some people ought to teach their dogs not to chase cars," one woman whined, "or else keep them to home. We might have gone into the ditch!"

Walter Ridge, custodian of McNeal Park, climbed into his rusted station wagon and slammed the door. It was mighty peculiar to him how Mary always thought of something she needed right now, every Monday night just five minutes before the only television program he really liked. As if the whole world was going to fall apart if she didn't get her liver sausage tonight. Couldn't wait till morning.

"I'm going to teach that woman to drive if it's the last thing I do," he muttered darkly. "Better have lights, I reckon. Gets dark so early anymore."

He drove toward town at a faster clip than usual. It was an hour long program, and if the Supervalue wasn't too crowded, he could still catch most of it.

Suddenly his headlights caught a flash of gold, and a big dog was in the road directly in front of him, feet planted firmly, barking wildly. He slowed and honked and pulled toward the other lane, but the dog moved with him. Puzzled, Walter coasted to a stop and stared at the dog. There hadn't been any cases of rabies around here recently, but you never knew. Still, something about the dog, a pleading quality in the barking, made him switch off the ignition and open the door a cautious crack. He could still slam it if the dog charged.

But Kate, having stopped the car, was across the road and down the ditch, then up again to bark at the man. Walter, being a curious man and basically unafraid of animals, got out and crossed the road. Then he saw the bicycle, and the girl, still unconscious.

"My Lord," he breathed, sliding haphazardly down the bank. He circled around the girl, saw that she was breathing, noted the pinch of denim caught in the bicycle chain. He started to pick her up, then stopped, remembering you're not supposed to move injured people. Quickly he scrambled up to the road, started the car into a screeching U-turn, and roared back toward his house just inside the park gate.

Kate, understanding dimly that things were out of her hands, lay down beside Robin, whimpering uneasily from time to time. She was still there when the ambulance arrived on the heels of Walter and Mary Ridge.

Mary, having had the presence of mind to bring scissors, cut Robin's slacks loose from the chain, and Walter gently worked the bike out from under Robin. Then the two ambulance men placed her on a stretcher. Kate stayed in the middle of things, as close to Robin as she could, while the stretcher was carried up the embankment and slid into the ambulance. Then, before they could stop her, she leaped in beside Robin. She crouched beside the girl and dared anyone to move her.

The two men in white looked at each other, and at the dog. They ordered her out, to no avail. "She can't ride in the ambulance," the driver said helplessly. "Absolutely no dogs in ambulances."

Walter Ridge was standing at the edge of the road, in the headlights of his car, examining an object he had just stepped on in the grass. A small, feminine-looking pair of brown glasses, broken in two.

With an air of authority, Mary Ridge stepped up to the ambulance, untying the sash of her cotton housedress. Reaching into the ambulance, she knotted the end through Kate's collar, patting the dog. "Come on, honey; you can ride in with us." The woman's round, lined face was wet with unashamed tears.

Reluctantly Kate stood, turning once to whimper at Robin; then she jumped down and followed the woman to the waiting car. She leaped into the front seat, between Walter and Mary Ridge, and sat, paws digging into the woman's ample lap, all the way through Cedar Grove to the hospital on the other side of town. During the ride, she never once looked away from the taillights of the wailing white ambulance.

When Robin woke up, it was late Tuesday morning. She lay with her eyes closed for a long moment, feeling the strange hardness of the bed and aware of unfamiliar sounds and smells. She knew where she was. In the hospital. Vaguely she remembered flying over the handlebars toward the culvert. And she seemed to remember waking up once in the night. Not quite waking up, but being aware of someone moving around her.

Her head ached so badly she could feel it all through her body, and there was something wrong with one leg. She opened her eyes, and immediately her mother and father were standing over the bed, smiling down tremulously at her.

"You're awake! How do you feel?"

158

"Don't move, honey; just lie still. You're going to be okay." They both spoke at once, interrupting each other.

"My head hurts," Robin moaned. Then as her vision cleared, she rose up on one elbow, wincing. "Is Kate okay?"

"She's fine." Mrs. Morgan smiled damply. "She ran out in the road and stopped a car to get help for you. Lie back down, honey. You have a slight concussion and a twisted ankle, and some bruises from the bicycle, but nothing broken."

Robin was awake enough now to hurt all over. She sank back into the pillow. Kate ran out in the road? To stop a car? For her?

"Tell me everything that happened," she said, closing her eyes.

Her parents retrieved the chairs they had been dozing in all night and pulled them close to the bed.

"The hospital called us about eight-thirty last night," Mrs. Morgan began. "Gracey Rohgen works in Admitting now, and she recognized you. Of course Dad and I were worried sick by then, your not being home for supper. You were still unconscious when we got here." Her red-rimmed eyes, dull with sleeplessness, began to mist up again. She batted the tears away and smiled at her own silliness, now that everything was going to be all right.

She took a big breath and continued. "Mr. Ridge, you know, the custodian out at the park? Well, he was on his way to town when Kate flagged him down. After he saw you, he went and called the ambulance, and he and his wife followed it to the hospital and brought Kate. I guess your bike is still out there," she added thoughtfully.

"You've been down here all night?" Robin opened her eyes long enough to look from one to the other. They nodded. "And Kate *rode* to the hospital in those people's *car*?" There was wonder in her voice. Again her parents nodded.

Then Robin remembered. The dog show! "Did they say how long I'll have to stay in here? And how soon I can walk on my leg?"

"The doctor said you'd have to stay a few days," her father said. "About the leg, I don't know, but probably not too long. It's just twisted. A couple of weeks maybe."

"It'll have to be sooner than that," Robin said firmly "The dog show is this Sunday."

Her parents exchanged a look and said nothing.

Luckily the hospital was lax about their visiting hours, or they would have had trouble with Paul. He was there, a gold and brown mum plant in his arms, fifteen minutes after school was dismissed.

"Hi, Rob," he said, setting the plant on the windowsill. He was at a loss for conversation, seeing her lying there, half of her forehead bandaged. And she didn't look like herself without her glasses. "How do you feel?" He pulled a chair up beside the bed and sat down.

"Fine. A little sore here and there. Thank you for the flowers. They're beautiful. How did you know I was here?"

"Your mom called the school and left a message for me. I'm going to bring you your books and assignments every day, so you can keep up with your work. How did it happen, anyway? Your mom's message didn't say very much."

Robin told him about the accident, and about Kate's stopping Mr. Ridge and riding in his car to the hospital.

"How do you like that!" He grinned wryly. "You and I beat our brains out for weeks trying to coax her into my car, and some perfect stranger comes along and gets the job done on the first try." They both laughed to cover their emotions as they thought about Kate, and when they stopped, they found they were holding hands.

"Where are your glasses?" Paul asked, getting back to safer ground.

"Broken, when I fell, I guess. Mother ordered another pair just like them."

"Oh. Gee, I guess this kind of shoots holes in the dog show plans, huh." He was genuinely sympathetic.

Robin sat up a little straighter and tried to look optimistic. "Maybe not. The doctor was in this afternoon and said I could probably go home Thursday and that I should be walking around some by the end of the week. My ankle's just twisted. I think if I rest real hard between now and then I should be able to make it okay. I may need your help, though, getting Kate out to Mr. Crissman's for her trim, and bathing her and stuff like that. You can still go to the show, can't you?"

"Oh sure. Only maybe we ought to take my car instead of riding with Mr. Crissman. Then there'd be room for you to lie down in the back seat and rest till we got there."

They spent the rest of the afternoon happily revising their plans for the dog show, ignoring the possibility that Robin might be in no shape for the trip.

SIXTEEN

On Thursday afternoon Robin was released from the hospital. She stood in the lobby beside her mother, who carried her plant and overnight bag, while Mr. Morgan gave the needed insurance information to the girl at the desk. The bandage on her head was reduced to a small patch now, and aside from a general weak feeling and her still-painful, bandaged right ankle, Robin felt good. She was determined to feel good, at least until after Sunday.

Her father joined them, offering his arm for support, and the family walked through the door into the bright October afternoon. The Morgan car was parked in the loading zone opposite the door, and in the back seat, panting and grinning, sat Kate.

Robin let go of her father's elbow and hobbled ahead of them to the car. There were happy tears in her eyes as she climbed awkwardly into the back seat, fending off the dog's wild welcome.

"Did you have any trouble getting her in the car?" she asked on the ride home, her arms tight around Kate's neck.

Mrs. Morgan twisted on the front seat, one hand steadying the mum plant. "Just a little, but we kept saying, 'Let's go get Robin,' and it seemed as if she understood." Her round face beamed.

Robin, surprised at her weakness after the trip home, was content to doze on the living room couch the rest of the afternoon, but she insisted on coming to the table for supper. Her appetite was good, and she was sure she'd be able to manage the trip to Des Moines Sunday. All she had to do was convince her parents. The doctor had told her to take it easy for a few days, but he hadn't said not to make any car trips. And he had told her to exercise the ankle as much as possible. Robin had all her arguments prepared, but decided not to bring up the subject till tomorrow night.

She recuperated as hard as she could all day Friday on the couch, with Kate lying on the floor beside her, or bringing her rubber rat to be tossed and retrieved. The dog had never looked better, her eyes bright, her coat gleaming with good health and brushing. Watching her, Robin was determined that Kate would be shown Sunday, somehow.

A few of the girls in her class stopped after school, and Paul came as soon as he was done at the dry cleaners.

"Come over tomorrow morning," Robin told him under her breath as he was getting up to leave. "We'll take Kate out to Crissman's to get trimmed unless the folks just absolutely say no. At least this time we can all ride in the car."

All evening Robin meant to bring up the question of the dog show, but somehow the time wasn't quite right. She kept putting it off until she fell asleep on the couch. When she woke up, the house was dark and quiet. Someone had pulled off her slippers and tucked a blanket over her. Sighing, she wriggled around to lie on her stomach, one arm trailing onto the rug. Kate snored softly, somewhere close.

Robin woke up, hobbled to her room to put on slacks and a clean white blouse, and was downstairs again in time to eat breakfast with her mother.

"Where's Dad?" she asked, dropping a slice of bread into the toaster.

"He went downtown to pick up your new glasses. Dr. Oberman put in a rush order, and they were supposed to be ready today. Want a scrambled egg this morning, honey? How are you feeling? You look so much better, dressed."

"Yes please on the egg, and I feel fine." Her head still ached, and she couldn't put her whole weight on her sore ankle, but these were minor things and not worth mentioning. Not this morning anyway.

She drank a glass of orange juice, then said casually, "Paul's coming over this morning to take Kate and me out to Mr. Crissman's to get her trimmed." She held her breath and fixed her eyes on the opened jar of grape jelly in the center of the table.

Her mother turned from the stove, an eggy fork in her hand. "You're not still planning on going to the dog show, are you?"

"Sure." She sounded much more confident than she felt. "It's only a couple of hours drive, and we can leave right after Kate's class. And I can just sit and watch while Paul gets Kate ready. The only time I'll have to do anything will be just for a few minutes in the ring. I can already walk well enough for that, and by tomorrow afternoon I'll be healed that much more." Her confidence left her. "Please, Mother, can't I? The entry fee is paid already, and Paul and I worked so hard getting Kate ready, and I really do feel fine."

Mrs. Morgan scraped the fork under the eggs, turning them, stirring, then scooping them out onto a plate. "Well, I don't know, honey. I'll have to talk it over with Dad." She sighed and said reluctantly, "I guess it would be okay to go out to Mr. Crissman's anyhow. We'll see what your father says, and how you feel after your ride this morning. But a dog show is nothing to ruin your health over. If there's any danger of its being too much for you, you'll just have to pass this one up. There'll be other dog shows you know, dear."

Paul's car turned in the driveway just then; Robin bolted the rest of her breakfast, whistled for Kate, and ran, half hopping, out to meet him. She wanted to get away before her father got back.

Kate followed them readily into the car, but insisted on sitting in the front seat where she could lean against Robin for moral support when the car started to move.

Again they found Mr. Crissman and Frank in the grooming room, this time working on three dogs. The two men stared in surprise at Robin's bandages.

"What happened to you?" they asked in unison.

Robin told them about the accident and Kate's change of heart about cars, passing lightly over her injuries.

"You still think you can make the show?" Frank asked.

She nodded.

Mr. Crissman frowned. "Think you can show her, with that leg?"

"Yes, I think so." From the tone of her voice it was clear that she didn't just think so, she *intended* to.

"In that case, we'd better get her trimmed." Mr.

Crissman lifted Kate to the table and went to work.

"Who's this?" Paul asked, motioning to the dog Frank was bathing. The two pups, now seven months old and full grown, were in cages in the corner, a heater turned on their wet fur.

Frank worked up a soapy lather over the dog's back. "This is Champion Copper Lane's Gold Strike. She's entered as a Special."

The name rang a bell in the back of Robin's mind. "Isn't that Kate's mother?"

Mr. Crissman said, "Umm, yes, I believe she is. I'd forgotten. She's the only one of our brood matrons who's in good coat right now, so we thought we'd bring her along. Try for a Best of Breed."

"Oh. What did you mean, 'entered as a Special'?" She turned back to Frank.

"That's any dog that's already a champion. The champions don't compete against the non-champions for points, since they don't need any. I guess they didn't have a Specials class at the match, did they? That's because nobody shows champions at a sanctioned match. Well now, if that'd been a real show, the male that beat Kate would have gone on to compete with all the golden retriever champions for Best of Breed. See?"

She guessed so. "That'll keep you two busy, showing three dogs, won't it?"

Mr. Crissman smiled over Kate toward his kennel man. "Frank and I are a pretty good team. We've shown a lot of dogs together in our day, haven't we, Frank?"

The little man grinned and nodded emphatically.

"Do you two still want to ride over with us in the morning?" Mr. Crissman asked.

"Maybe we'd better go in Paul's car," Robin said. "There'd be more room for me to stretch my leg out. But thanks a lot anyhow. And thanks very much for all the help, the trimming and all that."

"Not at all, not at all." He let Kate down from the table, and they all watched while she went to the tub to touch noses with the strange dog who was her mother, keeping a wary eye on Frank, who was hosing rinse water over Gold Strike.

"Doesn't look like the same dog you brought out here last summer," Mr. Crissman mused. "You've done a whale of a job with her. Just remember not to be disappointed if she doesn't win everything in sight tomorrow, though. Dog shows are a funny game, and there's no accounting for a judge's decision sometimes. Look us up as soon as you get there."

Robin was quiet on the ride home. Her head was aching dully, and she kept thinking how awful it would be, now that Kate was trimmed and beautiful, if her father said no to the trip tomorrow.

The Morgans were just sitting down to lunch when Robin and Paul got back. Forcing herself not to limp, Robin led the way through the back door into the kitchen.

"Back so soon?" Mrs. Morgan smiled at them. "We've got plenty of lunch if you'd like to stay, Paul. Do you like tuna casserole?" She reached for an extra plate.

"Yes, thank you." He followed Robin to the kitchen sink to wash up, and Kate flopped to the floor under the table.

"You're looking hale and hearty," Mr. Morgan said as his daughter hitched up her chair beside him. "By the way, here are your specs." He reached into the pocket of his flannel shirt and handed her the small packet.

The new glasses were identical to the broken ones, and they seemed oddly like long lost friends to Robin. She put them on and almost immediately her headache backed off a degree. Come to think of it, she reasoned, five days without them would give me a headache whether I had a concussion or not. The world brightened as the glasses brought it into focus again.

"You're looking hale and hearty," Mr. Morgan to that dog show tomorrow," Mr. Morgan said, dipping into the steaming casserole dish. "Why don't you all pass your plates and I'll dish up. Do you feel well enough for all that excitement, honey?"

"Oh yes. I feel perfectly normal. And with Paul and Mr. Crissman to help, I won't have to do a thing but lead Katy around the ring a few times. I know I can do it." She turned on all her persuasion.

170

He dished up another plate and started it around the table. "What do you think, Addy?"

"Well, I don't know. I hate to think of Robin's going off like that. . . ."

"Why don't you two come along?" Robin looked from one to the other, suddenly aware that they should have been included in the plans all along. "Then you can make sure I don't get too tired or anything. And besides, you might enjoy it, especially if Katy wins."

Her mother, who hadn't wanted to be the one to disappoint Robin, jumped at this excuse to approve. "I think it might be fun. What do you say, Dad?"

"All right, if Paul will drive. I'm not so good at highway driving anymore." He chuckled. Then, for no reason, everyone was laughing.

SEVENTEEN

It was a perfect blue and gold October day, cool enough for comfort but warm enough for shirt sleeves. At a little after noon, the pink and white Chevrolet drove under the high arched entrance to the Iowa State Fairgrounds. The broad avenue ahead was already lined with cars, station wagons, and vans of every description. To their right the Morgans and Paul could see the crowd around the Varied Industries Building. Paul drove as close to the building as he could, deposited his passengers, and left to find a parking place.

The Varied Industries Building was open on all four sides, leaving just a giant roof arching over brick pillars and a concrete floor. Down the center of the floor were six white-fenced squares back to back, and around them were crowds of people, some in folding chairs but most standing or moving about, amid clusters and stacks of dog crates. The crates were in varied sizes, wood and metal, fancy and nondescript. The crowds spilled out through the open walls onto the shaded lawn surrounding the building.

Robin was beginning to feel nervous again. Not so much as at the match, but enough to make her wish Kate's class was over so she could enjoy the show. She led the way around the rings, her parents close behind, until she saw Frank's familiar back. He had one of the pups standing on a crate in a corner of the building, getting a final going over with brushes and coat dressing.

"There you are," he greeted Robin. "We was afraid you might not make it. Howdy, folks." He extended his hand while Robin introduced her parents; then he motioned to one of the four matched crates, all bearing the Copper Lane insignia on their aluminum sides. "Why don't you put Kate in that crate there, till time to get her ready. You got a couple hours yet."

It was tempting. Kate's tugging at the lead was wearing Robin out already, and she longed to sit down somewhere. "I don't know if she'd stay in one. She'd probably get scared if I left her."

"Aw, she'll be okay," Frank insisted. "Look at her.

173

She don't look scared, does she? Put her in there, and you can set beside her if it'll make you feel any better."

Robin opened the crate door, and to her surprise Kate walked right in, turned around, and lay down, completely at ease. "I think I'll stay here awhile anyway," she said to her parents.

"Come on, Dad," her mother urged, looking around the building with lively interest. "Let's walk around a little. I saw some cocker spaniels over there that look just like Cindy."

When they had left, Robin pulled a folding chair over close to Kate's crate, where she could visit with Frank and still keep out of his way. People were milling all around them, some stopping to admire the pup Frank was combing, reaching out hesitant hands to pat him. The puppy leaned so far forward to get his pats that once or twice he nearly fell off the crate.

Paul found them at the same time that Mr. Crissman emerged from the crowd. "Good. You're here." Mr. Crissman extricated himself from a passing dachshund that had wrapped itself and its lead around his legs. "Beginning to worry about you. Had lunch yet?" The question included Paul and Frank.

Robin shook her head, and the four, with Mr. and Mrs. Morgan, whom they found beside the ring where the cocker spaniels were being judged, made their way to the far corner of the building, where tables had been set up. They had a long wait in the line to get their barbecued ribs and potato salad.

Robin ate carefully so as not to drip barbecue sauce on her new brown plaid wool skirt and deep brown sweater. The outfit had been bought with clinic earnings especially for this occasion because she thought it had the proper degree of sportiness, and because the pleated skirt would allow easy kneeling when she posed Kate. Also, she thought the colors would go well with a burnished golden retriever.

Glancing at his watch, Carter Crissman looked down the table at Robin. "We working people had better be getting our dogs groomed. Are you through eating?"

As they all made their way back toward their dogs, Mrs. Morgan asked, "Which ring will you be in?" Frank pointed it out, and the two senior Morgans dropped behind to look for chairs as close to that ring as possible.

Paul was pressed into service when they got back to the dogs. He brushed one of the two pups while Frank worked on the other, Mr. Crissman did Gold Strike, and Robin groomed Kate. There was much good-natured confusion and passing back and forth of brushes and combs. But finally all four retrievers were sprayed with coat dressing, polished down with palms of hands, and allowed to jump down from their crates.

"Just follow me," Mr. Crissman said, and the four handlers with their golden dogs fell into a line that wove around, between, and through bunches of noisy people and dogs, toward Ring Three.

Robin's stomach was bunchy now, and her hands moist, but it wasn't the old sick, scared kind of nervousness. In fact it was almost pleasant. She was actually looking forward to getting in there and doing her job. Her ankle had begun to ache a little, even when she wasn't stepping on that foot, but for such a short time in the ring she was sure it would be okay. She could even envision the people watching from ringside saying to one another, "Look at that poor girl out there, showing her dog, with a broken foot. Such a brave girl."

Mr. Crissman nudged her and motioned toward a balding young man who stood at the entrance to the ring, a booklet in one hand and a batch of cardboard armbands in the other.

"Do you know your number?" the man asked Robin.

"Nine."

"Oh yes." He crossed something off in the booklet and shuffled through the armbands, handing her one with a large black nine. She turned with it to Mr. Crissman, who was already wearing his on his left arm. He helped her on with hers, sliding it awkwardly over her sweater sleeve.

There was a class of pointers in the ring. It was the Specials class, Frank informed her, consulting his show catalog. "There's three Chesapeakes and one flat-coated retriever, then us," he said. "In goldens there'll be two Puppy Dogs, two Open Dogs, one Puppy Bitch, one Bred-by-Exhibitor Bitch, four Open Bitches—that's your class—and three Specials."

Robin could see her parents beaming at her from across the ring. They had managed to get front row seats.

The pointers were finished now, and the three dun-colored Chesapeake Bay retrievers were in the ring. The flat-coat was absent, someone informed the bald young man at the ring entrance. He nodded, made a notation, and spoke into a small metal instrument hanging from his belt.

"What's that?" Robin asked Mr. Crissman.

"Walkie-talkie. Keeps in contact with the announcer with it. See that fellow in the blue jacket up on the little platform over there? That's the announcer. The ring stewards call in to him which dogs are needed at each ring. Keeps the judging going smoothly."

"Golden retrievers eleven and twelve to ring three please," came the announcement. "All Maltese to ring one please; all Maltese, ring one. Basenjis to ring six. . . ."

Then suddenly Mr. Crissman and Frank were in the ring with the pups. Paul, holding Gold Strike, moved over close to Robin to watch as the two circled the ring.

The judge was a small, dapper gentleman in a

neat dark suit. His black and silver hair was waved back from an almost too elegant face, and his movements were quick and precise. Almost like a miniature movie star, Robin thought.

In almost no time the puppy Mr. Crissman led was designated the winner. The other classes followed in rapid succession, and Robin found herself in the ring with three other handlers, all men, and three other golden retrievers, all immaculately groomed and well-behaved. As they started around the rubber-matted square at a fast walk, Robin concentrated on not limping, keeping the lead high under Kate's neck, holding the dog's head up and her own arm straight out, watching the judge, and not running into the man ahead of her.

By the time the judge signaled a halt, her left arm was ready to drop off, and her ankle felt tender and puffy under the tight bandage. Copying the others, she slipped Kate's lead off and posed her, her right hand under Kate's chin, her left holding the tail out in place. She had to stretch her arms to reach, and in seconds her right arm was aching from lack of leverage. Kate must be resting her whole weight on her neck, she thought grimly. And the new sweater was hot and terribly itchy. Beneath her own discomfort, though, Robin realized that Kate was behaving very well. At least the dog didn't seem nervous. She held her stance and followed the judge with calm brown eyes.

One by one, the handlers were motioned out of the line and asked to gait their dogs diagonally across the ring, then across the end and back the same way, in a sort of figure seven. Robin was glad she was last in line. She watched the others carefully, cheering inside when one of the dogs alternately veered off the mat and sat down to be dragged. At the end of its solo gaiting, each dog was thoroughly examined.

When her turn came, Robin replaced Kate's lead and stood up, grateful for the chance to move. When she stepped forward, the bad ankle gave, and she stumbled. Blushing, she caught herself and went on, but the foot felt dead. She couldn't help limping, making Kate's normally smooth trot a little hesitant and jerky as she tried to stay beside her handler.

The judge was frowning when their figure seven was completed, but he said nothing as Robin set her dog up for his inspection. Kate held steady for him, even wagging her tail ever so slightly as he moved around her, seeing with his hands her bone and muscle structure.

When he was finished, he motioned for more circling, and around they went. Robin's foot was awake now, and hurting. Her face was damp; her glasses refused to stay up. After endless rounds, the judge's neat little hand went up, and the handlers and dogs alike stopped.

Resting her weight on her good leg, Robin tried surreptitiously to ease her bandaged foot out of its shoe for a moment. But the judge was motioning to her.

"Gait your dog again please, miss," he said in his precise voice. "Just up and back."

Robin was hobbling openly now and unable to keep a steady pressure on Kate's lead. At this point she didn't care so much about winning as just getting it over with.

"All right. You're one." As he spoke, the judge turned his back on Robin and wrote something in a black notebook on the little table behind him. The meaning of his words didn't sink into Robin's weary brain until he turned again, extending a blue ribbon to her.

He distributed the other ribbons while Robin stood aside in a happy fog. She waited on one foot, catching her breath and grinning at Paul and Mr. Crissman, then turned to smile at her parents who were busily informing their neighbors that that was their daughter in there with the blue ribbon.

Then the winners of the Puppy and Bred-by-Exhibitor classes were called back to the ring to compete with Kate for Winners Bitch. This is the important one, Robin reminded herself. This is going for the championship points now. She gritted her teeth and led out around the ring.

In a mercifully short time the judge made his decision and with a perfunctory smile handed the purple and white Winners ribbon to Robin. She'd won the points! Kate was really on her way to being a champion now! Robin felt a little dizzy, but she couldn't leave the ring yet. There was still Best of Winners.

With some surprise she saw Mr. Crissman in the ring with one of the pups. Then she remembered he had won Winners Dog. This will end it, she thought. Mr. Crissman is a pro.

They repeated the circling and posing. By now Robin's whole right leg was on fire, and it was all she could do to get around the ring. Her glasses were riding halfway down her nose, and her head was splitting.

The judge was not so quick to decide this time. He scowled back and forth between the flashy but immature pup and the mature dog who was probably the better of the two . . . if only he could get a clear picture of her gait. The girl was obviously doing her best with a game foot, but the dog's slow, choppy gait, caused by the girl's limp, could be camouflaging faults in body structure that he hadn't seen.

"Change dogs please, and gait number nine."

Mr. Crissman and Robin exchanged quick looks; then Robin numbly handed him Kate's lead and took the pup's. The judge motioned her to stay where she was, while Mr. Crissman stepped out briskly with Kate. Robin watched anxiously, but Kate seemed not to care who was on the other end of her lead. She moved out proudly, head and tail high, watching

Robin from the corner of her eye.

"That's enough, thank you. Take your own dogs please." Satisfied that Kate's only gaiting problem was her handler, the judge marked his little book, "Best of Winners, Number Nine."

Robin moved to the ring entrance to hand her three ribbons to Paul, while Mr. Crissman exchanged his pup for Gold Strike, whom Frank was holding ready.

"There'll be a slight delay," the balding ring steward informed them. "One of the Specials isn't here yet. The handler is tied up in another ring."

The judge poured himself a glass of water at his table, Mr. Crissman struggled to change armbands one-handed, and Robin sank into a chair beside the ring entrance. All at once she knew she couldn't go another step, and there was still Best of Breed. Her leg was a stump of pain, and the room was beginning to tip. . . .

EIGHTEEN

Before she could faint, Robin was nearly jarred out of her chair by a snarling yellow body thrashing against her. The two Crissman pups, heretofore best friends, had both spotted a bit of dried liver someone had dropped on the floor. Frank, who had been holding both their leads in one hand and looking over the crowd for the absent dog, snapped to and began trying to untangle the two leads and keep the dogs from getting at each other. Paul grabbed the nearest pup, and in a second the leads were untangled.

"Help me get these scallywags back in their crates, will you?" Frank muttered, and he and Paul disappeared in the crowd with the abashed pups, neither of whom had gotten the liver.

Mr. Crissman grinned wryly after them, then noticed Robin's face. "Look here, young lady," he scolded, "you look like grim death, and you can't give your dog a fair showing in that condition. I can get someone else to take her in this next class for you. I'd show her myself if I didn't have Goldie. How about it?"

Someone else show Kate? It was unthinkable, and yet Robin didn't know how she'd ever get through another workout in there without passing out completely. She weighed it in her mind, quickly and painfully. Kate would have a better chance with someone else showing her, but then the victory wouldn't be Robin's. And maybe Kate *wouldn't* do better for someone else. Maybe she wouldn't let anyone but Robin handle her. But she just had, Robin reminded herself. She just let Mr. Crissman . . .

"Maybe Frank could, or Paul." She looked up at Mr. Crissman and tried to be matter of fact about handing Kate over to someone else. But the dog that had been delayed was there now, and there was no time to wait for Frank or Paul.

"Hey, Carl. Carl Sanders. Are you busy?" At Mr. Crissman's hail, a pleasant-looking elderly man who had been walking by turned and came toward them, a smile of recognition lighting his face.

"Carter, good to see you, you old . . ."

"No time for pleasantries." Mr. Crissman's smile

184

took the edge off the words. The rest of the class was in the ring, and the judge was looking at them. "Would you do us a favor and take this dog in? Got a sick little handler here."

The old face wrinkled into a broad grin, and he winked down at Robin. In a flash he was slipping on her armband and taking Kate's lead from her hand. "Sure thing. What's the dog's name?"

"Kate."

"Come along, Katy, my dear." He followed Mr. Crissman into the ring, and the judge started them circling immediately. Robin watched numbly; things had happened so fast. Then Paul and Frank were back.

"My leg gave out," she explained in answer to their startled looks. "Mr. Crissman got him to show Kate." She waved vaguely toward the ring. Across the expanse she saw two empty chairs where her parents had sat, and before that had time to register, Mr. and Mrs. Morgan were beside her, fluttering and demanding to know what was wrong.

"Nothing. My leg just got too tired." Suddenly Robin was so weary she could barely stay upright in the chair. She turned back to the ring and tried to make her mind focus.

Kate was doing very well, she noted with mixed feelings. Evidently Mr. Sanders knew what he was doing.

"He's one of the best," Frank murmured. "Pro-

185

fessional handler, retired now, but he can't stay away from the shows."

The other dogs were showing beautifully, too, though, and Robin knew that Kate's chances against three champions, all professionally groomed and handled, were almost nil. But she was very, very proud of her dog, in spite of the fact that Kate was performing for someone else. From the sidelines Robin was able to get a much better view of Kate, and she honestly couldn't see that the others were any better.

Even though she didn't expect Kate to win, Robin felt a keen stab of disappointment when the judge, with theatrical drama, pointed to one of the other dogs and handed the tall silver trophy to the dog's handler. She was working hard at composing her face like a good sport when she saw the judge hand another ribbon to Carl Sanders and drop a friendly pat on Kate's head.

Robin twisted around to look up at Frank. "I thought there was no second place for Best of Breed."

"There ain't. That was Best Opposite Kate got. Best of Opposite Sex to Best of Breed. The dog that won was a male, so that means the judge picked Kate over the other two champions, who in this case were both females. See?"

"You mean Kate won over Gold Strike? And that other champion?"

Frank grinned. "Yep. Even beat her old lady."

The dogs were out of the ring now, and Kate was scrambling to hoist her sixty bulky pounds into Robin's lap.

"You got a heck of a good dog here." Mr. Sanders handed over Kate's lead. "She shows like a trooper, too, except she kept wanting to look over this way."

"You didn't think she acted . . . timid?" Robin hugged Kate and looked over her at Mr. Sanders.

"Timid! If she'd been timid, she'd never have got Best Opposite in that kind of competition, girlie. Well, excuse me, got to go see a man about a dog."

"Thank you for showing her," Robin called after his retreating back.

"Well, young lady, you've got yourself four points. Eleven more and Kate's a champion. Not a bad afternoon's work, especially for an old crippled lady. How do you feel now?" Mr. Crissman was smiling down at her just as though she hadn't just beaten his dog.

"I feel great. Just great." She beamed at him and Paul and her parents. And Kate.

"You know," he said thoughtfully, "it's quite a compliment to you, Robin, that Kate let a stranger take her like that, and performed for him. It's one thing to make a shy animal trust and depend on you, and quite another thing to make her unafraid of the rest of the world. Quite another thing entirely. If you folks are ready to start for home, may I suggest we meet, say, at the Ox Yoke Inn at Amana? I'd like

187

to buy dinner and celebrate this young lady's win."

Everyone agreed, and Paul helped Robin up. Mr. Crissman and Frank went back to their dogs, and the Morgans, Paul, and Kate made their way toward the car. Paul's arm was around Robin's waist, supporting her as they followed her parents out, and Kate wagged along beside Robin, dimly aware that she had done something well.

THE MIDNIGHT FOX

by Betsy Byars

illustrated by Ann Grifalconi

Tom didn't want to spend the summer on his Uncle's farm. But his parents were going to Europe and he had no choice.

One day, Tom saw the wild black fox and it was the most awesome sight he'd ever seen. He knew that his whole life, his whole world, would be changed. Then, during the most terrible night of his life, Tom had to find a way to save the wonderful black fox and her baby.

AVON CAMELOT BOOK
46987 $1.50

Also by Betsy Byars
AFTER THE GOAT MAN   41590 $1.25
THE 18th EMERGENCY   46979 $1.50
RAMA THE GYPSY CAT   41608 $1.25
THE SUMMER OF THE SWANS   46961 $1.50
TROUBLE RIVER   47001 $1.50
THE WINGED COLT OF CASA MIA   46995 $1.50

Winner of the Newbery Medal

THE SUMMER OF THE SWANS

by Betsy Byars

illustrated by Ted CoConis

What had changed in Sara she did not know. Her moods were as unaccountable as the sudden appearance of the swans which so fascinated Charlie, her mentally retarded younger brother, as he watched them glide silently across the lake.

Suddenly, one night, Charlie disappeared—and Sara's own miseries were left behind as she searched for Charlie, who wandered somewhere, lost, helpless, and bewildered. Sara turned to Joe Melby, and together they found him. The longest day of the summer was over, and Sara knew she would never be quite the same.

An Avon Camelot Book
46961 $1.50

Also by Betsy Byars
AFTER THE GOAT MAN   41590 $1.25
THE MIDNIGHT FOX   46987 $1.50
RAMA THE GYPSY CAT   41608 $1.25
TROUBLE RIVER   47001 $1.50
THE WINGED COLT OF CASA MIA   46995 $1.50

A suspenseful mystery with a surprise ending!

THE CHRISTMAS TREE MYSTERY

by Wylly Folk St. John

Beth Carlton was in trouble. She accused Pete Abel of stealing the Christmas ornaments from her family tree, something she knew he hadn't done. And what was worse—the police believed her! Beth had two days to prove to the police that Pete wasn't a thief, and all she had to go on was her stepbrother's word that Pete was innocent.

An Avon Camelot Book
46300 · $1.50

Avon Camelot Books are available at your bookstore. Or, you may use Avon's special mail order service. Please state the title and code number and send with your check or money order for the full price, plus 50¢ per copy to cover postage and handling, to: AVON BOOKS, Mail Order Department, 250 West 55th Street, New York, New York 10019. Please allow 4-6 weeks for delivery.